The Synchronicity Code

Lazlo Ferran

The Synchronicity Code

Lazlo Ferran

PRINTING HISTORY

First Edition

Printed in 12 point Times New Roman

This is a work of fiction. Names, characters, places and incidents are products of the author's imagination or are used fictitiously and should not be construed as real. Any resemblance to actual events, locales, organisations or persons, living or dead, is entirely coincidental.

Published by Future City Publishing, London.

Cover: OmriKoresh.com

Acknowledgments

Thanks to Pedro, Hugh, Kris, Derek and Luxmi.

Contents

Chapter One 11

Chapter Two 43

Chapter Three... 81

Chapter Four.. 105

Chapter Five 133

Chapter Six... 167

Appendix 227

Biography of Lazlo Ferran 231

'Spirit! that dwellest where,
In the deep sky,
The terrible and fair,
In beauty vie! –'

– Edgar Allan Poe

Chapter One

My name was Byron Monk. I was found dead this morning in the Waterfall Café Motel, hanging from the ceiling.

My hand and feet were nailed to the ceiling and a silver stake had been driven through my heart. Silvia was lying on the bed, half asleep, with her back turned to my corpse.

It's only the third time I have been killed. When prepared, a vampire as old as I can cheat death, but I still had to run.

My next stop would be Jerusalem, AD 30. That's where I met the old werewolf, although at first, I only saw a white-haired stranger, who wore 20th Century cologne and crouched vomiting under dripping, crimson-dyed cloths in Market Street.

I took him to a wine house and asked him for his story. I soon wished I hadn't. Having just cheated my own death, I wasn't so curious about the bad dream he had had the night before; a horse with emerald eyes whipping his murdered daughter, who walked among a circle of girls in Hell. I was more interested in what he said had happened in the morning:

"I parked the car under a full moon near Corbie. An old oak, which I hadn't seen for an eon, still marked the spot. Candlelight cast eerie, dancing shadows upon the leaves and twelve gorgeous, naked girls who were dancing in a large circle. The music stopped. A girl went to an altar stone in the centre. A man pulled back her blonde hair and put a sword to her neck.

"'Welcome John!' He shouted to me, 'Do you want your pleasure? It's yours!' I yelled, 'Stop!'

"I leaped forward to save the girl. She turned and smiled at me. Her look was ecstatic. Before I could reach her, she lifted her face, and he sliced through her neck … .

"A mad panic took me. I ran, away from the horror. For a moment, I had *wanted* to kill that girl, taste the lust I had seen in her eyes. *You*, of all people, know what it is to lust after blood. But to escape what I wanted the most, I could only run to what I had lost; my murdered daughter, Annie, and the closest thing to her, Georgina."

"I met Georgina while chasing my daughter's murderer, a Biblical Serpent who can slip through the cracks of time and space. It put her up to seduce me. But I discovered that she loved me when she saved me from the Serpent

"I have heard of them … ."

"Later still, when I had rescued my marriage, Georgina kidnapped my wife, and I had to follow her, through time, to the 13th Century. This time I had to rescue my wife, but it seems that Georgina wouldn't harm her anyway, because of her love for me. The Serpents punished her for her reluctance by sending her here, now. But with my wife gone, and after what I saw in Corbie, I have to find Georgina and *save* her."

"You see, she *looks* like my daughter. She has the same, wild spirit which I used to see in my daughter's eyes. She is what Annie might have been, had she grown up. They even sound … sounded alike. But she will only have less than a day to live … ."

The old werewolf sounded desolate. It's not my style to touch a man in sympathy, but I felt his pain, lost as he was in the vaults of time. He went on:

"Coming as far as we do, from the 20th Century, I am told we can survive here only for days, and there is *no* way back!"

I nodded.

"I might have a few more days than her, three at

most. We lose nineteen years of age every day. I *have* to find her fast!"

"Well, right now, I think we have to leave. We're being watched!" I told him. "Look!"

A tall figure, wearing a black kudra or headscarf, bound with rope bands, which were braided with blue and gold cords, watched us from a shaded portion of the raucous room. I couldn't see his eyes, the only part of his face not covered, because he had glanced away when I looked at him.

"What do I call you?" I asked as I led the werewolf to the doorway.

"John. Did you see those eyes?"

"They can't be as distinctive as yours, one blue and one brown. Do you have somewhere to stay?"

"I told you. I just arrived when you found me."

"I thought so. You didn't tell me how you knew you should come to Jerusalem? Or how you know how long you have? Better tell me now. It's safer while we walk. Even the inn walls have ears here. Follow me."

"I used what I call a 'Gate,' a time portal of some kind, to get here. There are only a few, and the only one that leads to this period comes out in Jerusalem! As for how long I have to live, I had another dream or something. Another witch, Herleva … ."

"Don't tell me. You are in love with her too?"

"Well, it's not like that but … she helped me."

I led him past twisting streams of donkeys, merchants, carrying their wares and citizens of the bustling city, down a backstreet into the impoverished Lower City. Each time I turned round, John seemed to have fallen behind. I turned to the right and waited for him.

"Up here!" I told him, starting up a steep side street.

We reached the neighbourhood of my inn. I stopped at my favourite stall and paid for a loaf of flat bread, goat's cheese, some olives and a pot of wine. I wasn't poor, but being inconspicuous was the name of the game.

I led the stranger through an arch and into a small, tidy courtyard.

"Round the back," I explained.

"I thought I saw those eyes again, while you were at the stall. Very strange … ."

"Why?"

Beautiful, almond shaped, emerald green. I could swear it was a woman."

"Every kind of stranger washes up here eventually," I told him, exiting the property through another arch and turning left into a shaded street, like a cleft. "Quick. Run, just in case." I strode ahead while John had to run to keep up. "But women don't dress as merchants *or* go to wine houses. Never!"

"Maybe."

I turned right again, stepped under yet another arch and entered another courtyard, pocked with goat's ordure.

"Round the back?" John ventured.

I began to climb a flight of steps up the rear of the white-painted stone of the inn.

"I thought, you know, people like you, aren't supposed to like the sun," John said.

"It's a myth," I told him as I pulled aside the blue cloth sheet covering the doorway. "I don't like the sun, and after a while, it does break down our skin cells. I wouldn't want to be under a hot sun more than a few hours. But in April, it's not too bad. Take a seat."

"Seventh of April, to be precise. The day before Passover. Do you know what that means?"

"It means you are lucky. The wine houses are only open during festivals. If I hadn't been able to drag you to a noisy one to recover, somebody worse than a merchant might have seen us.

"No. Fine. That's not what I meant! Jesus is due to be crucified tomorrow. *That's* what I meant!"

***

John's mention of Iesous made me start. He had hit on the main reason I was there. Was it coincidence? I decided to conceal my feelings.

"So how are you going to find her, this Georgina?" I asked. "Where is she likely to be?"

"Likely to be *soon*. She doesn't get here for another two days."

"Oh great. So you are looking for somebody who isn't even here yet! And you only have three days to live?"

Three days. It's not long to live. I should walk away from this situation. I can't help him. I don't have time.

I opened my mouth to speak, but John smiled at me with a mouthful of bread and cheese. I hesitated, and then it was too late. I was caught.

"This is great but … do you have fresh blood?" John asked.

"That's not a problem."

"But not human blood."

"I don't drink human blood. I never … . Never mind. Why do you need it now?"

"It helps when using the Gate, but I didn't have time … ."

"You didn't have time to arrange your clothes either!" I replied. "We have to get you something more appropriate. I'll go and get the blood in a few minutes, and while I am out, I will find something for you to wear. You are attracting too much attention already with that white skin. *Where* did you get that?"

"It's a kaftan, from Africa. It was all I could find in 19th Century London."

"Wait here. I will be back soon."

When I returned from the butcher with two gourds of blood, John was staring out of the window.

"An archaeologists dream!" Look at it! And yet I don't have time to enjoy it. I have to find Georgina."

"Yes. And you didn't tell me how you expect to do that."

"No. I know she will be held by Serpents. They can take human form. I am guessing at least one of them will be posing as somebody powerful here. They are too vain to pose as anything else."

"Well that helps a lot!" I told him.

"But I will know when I see one."

"Drink the blood and change into this. Then I am prepared to search the bazaars with you for a while. Tonight, I have my own challenge."

"What is that?"

"I will tell you later."

The stranger struck me as weary of life, resourceful, and I could see in his eyes that he had done some fighting, the kind you do in wars. He was more passive than I, but this concealed something, something lethal. He was dangerous. He was also an intellectual, something I liked very much in others. There was a lot to like about him. And he was a werewolf.

A resourceful fellow.

"What is your full name?" I asked him. "We may as well get this over with.

"John Rezor. And you?"

"You can call me Byron Monk if you prefer, but my original name is Zosimyache."

"Greek. Interesting. I'm ready. Shall we go?"

After he had wiped his mouth clean of blood and put on his white kudra to match the simlah I had bought him I led him out through the back of the courtyard and into a shaded street.

"The sandals are okay?" he asked.

"You mean the footwear? As long as nobody looks too closely, they will pass. I am taking you to the Upper Market, a good place to start. Today is market day so many of the rich will go there."

"How much do I owe you for the clothes? I brought gold instead of money, jewellery mostly."

"Forget it. We will exchange some of your gold for coins at the market."

As we climbed up the sloping streets, myself wearing a black kudra, few even glanced at us.

"Are there usually this many soldiers?" John asked, glancing at a centurion.

"No. There are more than usual, even for Passover. The City has been tense for days now."

We walked toward Herod's Palace in the north-west corner of the City. Every pavement and street corner was crammed full of busy traders, customers and stalls, selling food, wine, beer from Egypt, every type of cloth and garment.

"What's that?" John asked, pointing to a tower, topped with a four-sided pyramid.

"King David's tomb."

John seemed to fall behind, and I caught him looking at the faces of poorer citizens. A few streets later, we passed from the squalor of the Lower City into the Upper where the streets were more orderly and less busy.

"And that's the Temple!" John exclaimed, looking enormous block of a building to the right.

"That's right. We are near the Upper Market now. Tell me if you smell anything."

"Smell? Oh, I see. Alright."

The dust of the unpaved Lower City streets was absent here. I wiped a crust of it from my mouth, just as we arrived in the Market. Roman, two-storey arcades formed three sides of an open space, which was filled with stalls. The distillers of expensive oils and perfumes; the master tailors and silk merchants; the goldsmiths and silversmiths; the dealers in ivory, incense and precious stones were all here.

While John took in the faces, my eye was caught by a pretty leg with an anklet of bells. The girls offering themselves here were not as fine as those in Athens, but they were still more interesting to me than anything else for sale. I am vain, it's true, and I wear jewellery, but craftsmanship can be copied while female beauty cannot.

"Where do we exchange the gold?" John whispered. I was just about to ask him why he was whispering when he added, "And I need to buy some weapons. What do you recommend?"

"Let's get the money first."

I led him to a goldsmith. and John showed him a fine necklace, four bracelets and two rings, one set with a diamond. The goldsmith didn't reply but announced:

"I can offer you two minas for the lot!"

He dropped the jewellery on the table without a glance and continued to work on an exquisite torque. John pulled me aside to whisper:

"How much is a mina?"

"In 2022 it would be about £50. I don't know, in your time. I haven't been there. About the price of a good meal for one person.

"No less than five," John told the goldsmith, picking up his items. He put them in his pocket, and the craftsman glanced up from his work.

"I can't offer you that. Taxes are extortionate here, and my wife is expecting. You are a soldier, are you not?" John coughed before turning to me:

"Does it show that *much*?"

"The way you walk, hold yourself. I can see you have fought."

"I could tell," I concurred.

"If you bring me your sword, I will decorate the hilt with gold thread for free," the goldsmith continued. It will be the finest work you have ever seen!"

"Four minas," John replied.

"You are joking, my friend. I am the best goldsmith in Jerusalem, perhaps in Judea. I tell you what, since I need to get on with my work, three minas. That is my final offer. If that is no good, go away."

"Three and three quarters."

I whispered in John's ears, "Three minas and thirty-eight shekels."

I was quite surprised when the goldsmith said, "Three and a half," grinning about his own currency joke. John handed the goldsmith the jewellery, and the craftsman gripped his hand.

"Well done!" I told John. "Maybe he though you are rich."

"Perhaps. Now for the weapons."

As I led John to the armourer his gaze shifted to the rooftops.

"What sort of situation are you contemplating?"

"Close combat, some of it outside and some inside."

"Then I suggest a sword *and* dagger."

We found an armourer, and he showed us a fine selection of jewelled swords and daggers. John picked up a dagger with a jewelled, gold handle but soon put it down. He selected a plain looking, straight blade and hefted it before placing it in my palm.

"Inexpensive but a serviceable blade," I told him.

He chose a similar sword, and again I approved.

The armourer was disappointed with his 50 shekels.

I followed John back to the goldsmith.

"Can you have it ready by tomorrow?" John asked, handing him the sword.

The craftsman hefted the weapon before replying:

"Come at midday."

***

We walked around the Market a little while longer. It was just past noon, so the streets became quieter for a while. I told John to conceal the dagger; Roman soldiers didn't appreciate weapons being on show in the City. John's glance often turned to the poor rather than any rich merchant or dignitary.

"Why do you look at *them*?" I asked.

"Oh, it's nothing. Just wondered if we might see someone."

"Iesous?"

"If that's what *you* call Christ, yes. He *could* be here. Earlier, he would have been by King David's Tomb."

"I don't know that much, but I have seen him."

"Where? When?"

"We should head back. Follow me," I told him. "I will take you past the place. I heard about his outburst in the Temple a week ago, but I didn't catch up with him until two days ago, outside a synagogue near here. He was criticising the Pharisees and the cast of Scribes. By the time I arrived, a huge crowd was filling the streets. I had to push my way through to hear him. I barely caught a glimpse of him. He was eloquent and had a powerful voice."

Somebody grabbed my sleeve from behind.

"Wait!" John said. I spun round, and he held on to my arm but stood stock still, as if sniffing the air.

"Something?" I asked.

"Something," John affirmed, after drawing a long breath. "Over there. What is that?"

He was pointing to one of the more opulent buildings, a two storey, white-plastered building with a courtyard within. The sound of carousing could be heard within.

A wine house of some kind, I don't doubt," I replied. "We wouldn't be admitted. It's for the rich only."

"Let's try. I 'smell' something, as you put it.

"If you insist but … ."

It was too late. John was already almost to the gate. I hurried after but only caught up when we stood at the door to a noisy bar. A tall, swarthy guard glared down at us and said:

"You can't come in."

A friend of his, no smaller, tapped him on the shoulder and he bent to listen.

"Today is your lucky day," he told us. A wicked smiled passed across his face, which didn't give me confidence. However, there was no stopping John.

Reckless!

The room's windows were covered and only dancing candlelight lit the room. We sat at a long bench, near the back of the room. Several half-covered faces turned to look at us before returning their attention to their drinks and the girl dancing in a small, open space at the front of the room. If the welcome had been warmer, I could have been happy. We were served two complimentary goblets of wine by another beautiful girl. She was dressed, in carefree mockery, as a merchant; in wide leggings and a red and white striped simlah. What gave away her sex was a veil instead of a kudra and a pretty pair of shins.

"Very good," I said, after sipping the wine. "I don't know … ." I didn't say anymore, because when I looked at John, he had frozen. He hadn't touched the wine.

"What's wrong?" I asked.

He didn't move for nearly a minute. I was feeling for my dagger hilt under my simlah, when he spoke:

"That girl. Those were the eyes I saw in the other bar. But I felt … I felt like a Serpent was in the room but maybe something even more powerful than *that*! I felt frozen and burned at the same time!"

Various girls presented themselves to dance before the audience. Some were appreciated by the discerning audience while others, not so much.

"I think you were imagining those almond-shaped eyes," I told John, who seemed to have relaxed.

"Perhaps I was wrong. Even so, I still feel something. You can go if you like."

"What and miss all these lovely females?"

"There!" John said, eyes wide.

I followed his gaze. I could see that the new girl to arrive on the dance floor was the same girl who had served us. We had been seated then. Now I could see that she was exceptionally tall and almost muscular, but her beauty was considerable. She moved like a tigress. John was even more agog than I.

"Who is she?" I said, half to myself.

"I don't know," John answered. Can we call her over?"

"Perhaps. When she has finished."

The dancing girl's almond-shaped eyes held each of ours for a moment near the end of the dance, and finally she removed her veil before leaving the stage. A large, green emerald hung over her nose.

"Unusual," I whispered.

But when we asked a serving girl if we could meet the tall dancing girl, she shook her head and left us.

"We should go," I suggested. I don't like this place.

"But I need to speak to her."

"Well my friend, if you really must, then I suggest later. These places don't really become busy until late at night. *Then*, you may have more luck."

"What is the name of this place? John asked"

"I will ask the guard."

"The Sweet Urn," I told John, when I caught him up

outside. He seemed distracted for a moment but then shook his head before saying:

"Right. Show me where you saw Jesus talk."

Close to the synagogue, I turned to John:

"Don't turn around. We're being followed. Forget the synagogue."

"Okay. What now?"

"You're a dangerous man to have as a friend!"

"Maybe they are from the The Sweet Urn?"

"Maybe. At the bottom of this hill is a very busy market. We'll lose them there. Hang on to my sleeve, and keep up. I may run.

"But I can't run too run far."

"Nonsense. You look a lot younger already!"

At the market, I led John through throngs of people between bustling stalls, twisting this way and that until I felt sure we would have lost the two men in anonymous white kudras. I led John out of the market through a series of narrow alleyways and back streets and then back toward my room. I had the strong urge to suggest to John that now he had money, he might like to lodge alone, but for some inexplicable reason, the idea made me feel guilty.

Damn!

***

"You have a lot of explaining to do!" I told John as soon as we were safely within my room. "I have been here for nearly a month, and this is the first time I have been followed! There's a lot of things about you that don't make sense. And then you claim a girl with green eyes is in a wine house, drinking with men *and* also a dancing girl!"

"It *is* the same woman. I'm sure of it now. Listen, I will explain everything, but I haven't slept for more than a day. Wake me an hour before you go out and I will tell you *everything*!"

"Fine."

"Oh, and can you please mix this wine with some water. I can't go on drinking *nothing* but wine!"

"Fine."

While John slept, I went over the day's events, but my mind slipped back one of my earliest memories. I had just learned to read and write and was day-dreaming next to a malotera bush on a plateau of Mount Othri. The sun was intoxicating, and the wind sung to me, but instead of sleeping, I turned to stare at a naked rock. As I looked, I thought I could see markings on it. I crept closer to the rock, which was about my size. I could discern something with wings and words in a language I couldn't read. I closed my eyes and saw demons flying in the night.

From that day forth, my innocence was lost. My parents barely had to teach me how to live as a vampire, because I instinctively knew what to do. My search has not been for truth but for light.

My thoughts returned again to the events of the day with John. I still couldn't make sense of it when he woke, shortly after sunset.

"So long do you have?" John asked.

"There is time. I am listening."

"Well, what do you want to know? I don't know who the two men were, following us. I really don't. And I know no more than you do about the girl. But didn't you feel something in The Sweet Urn?"

"I felt something, yes. Fear. There is something bad about the place." John nodded. "Start at the beginning. How did you meet this Georgina?"

"It's a long story. I will give you basics for the early stuff. I was a 'secret agent during the Second World War. You have heard of *that*?"

"Yes. I was born far in the past, but I needed to go to

2022 to find out a lot about history. Your methods are a lot better there. But this isn't about me."

"Right. I met my wife, Rose, during the War. She was an agent too, and we settled down in France where we had a boy and girl. The boy has long since grown up and had a son of his own, but my daughter, Annie, was murdered by a Serpent that came from a crack in the sky. I lost her, and my wife blamed me. Let me see … . About the same time, I became aware that there was something odd about my grandfather. I began to investigate some wolf statues I had, because they came from Bulgaria and Romania, a place where, my grandfather told me, our family originates. The Serpent murdered others beside my daughter, always moving north, toward Paris. I followed it there, and Georgina found me. It didn't quite happen like that, but basically, that's what happened. She knew about Rose but became my lover. I know now she seduced me. Then I found out she was being chased by a cult of Catholic assassins called the Concilium Putus Visum, the CPV."

I was trying to find out what happened to Annie, partly to save my marriage and partly my sanity. Then Georgina was murdered, or I thought she was. I was blamed for her death, so then I was being chased by the French police *and* the Serpents and the CPV, who, for some reason had first protected me and now wanted me dead! It turned out, they all wanted one thing, a ceremonial silver sword that could kill the Serpent."

I must have shuddered, because John went on:

"Oh sorry! I forgot. I will avoid mentioning silver! Anyway, Georgina came back to life and helped me kill the Serpent, clear my name and save my marriage."

But the Serpents arranged for the CPV to help Georgina kidnap my wife years later and take her back to the 13th Century, and even further back, to the 7th Century. I had to save her. Herleva, a witch, if you want to call her that, in the 13th Century, helped me. It was she who taught me that my family was one where alternative generations were werewolves. She taught me how to be one. Anyway, I caught up with Georgina and had to fight a giant knight to save my wife. Just when I was about to kill him, he turned into a Serpent and I into a werewolf. We fought, and I defeated him. I left Georgina with a cross cut into her belly. I couldn't kill her, because she had not been able to kill my wife!"

"Why?"

"Because she loves me!"

"Oh yes, I forgot. What then?"

"Until a few days ago, not much! My wife died, and by this time I had become an archaeologist of some reputation. So I organised a dig on a ruin of a Roman villa I had discovered while in the 13th Century."

The night before we left, I had a dream; the one I told you about the horse with emerald eyes. That girl has emerald eyes … ."

"True. But that means nothing. Go on with your story."

"I had another dream, later that night. Herleva was telling me that there was still time to save Georgina, that I had to go through a Gate in 19th Century London to 1st Century Jerusalem and that I would have three days to find her. I cheated. I used the Gate in such a way to arrive early, before Georgina has even arrived, even though she left years ago in my time."

"Extraordinarily understanding, your lovers! Like a little harem! But I don't understand why you are here *now*, at *this time*. You know the significance of today?"

"Yes. Jesus will be tried tonight and crucified tomorrow. Or at least that is what the Bible says."

"You are not sure?"

"Well, I haven't studied it, and I am not what you would call a good Christian, but all the evidence points to today. It's the best bet … . Is that why you are here?"

"Wait. You first. Why did your Herleva send you now?"

"I have thought about *that*. I don't know! Perhaps there is some connection with Georgina. I really don't know."

"Hm. Alright. My story? It's a lot simpler than yours! I was born in Greece, about a thousand years before this time. We were vampires, so we lived apart from men, in the hills. We sometimes had to steal sheep to live. I left my family early to find answers. But all I found out was that I was good with a sword. I fought in many wars before becoming wealthy, for a mercenary. When I returned to my home, I could find no sign of my family.

"I left that place and never went back. I fought in many wars, always for money. After perhaps an eon of time, I became weary of my life. I needed something to believe in. I searched all the religions of this world for meaning but found none. Then I heard of the Nazarene. I came here, but there was confusion and war. Nobody knew what to believe about him. I decided I would like to meet him. I can travel in time too. It's not like your Gates, more like running in a dream. I tried several times to come here at a time when I could speak with the Nazarene, but each time I failed. Life went on for a while, but you could barely call it a life. I fought with the Romans and later the Vikings, as you call them, and later still, in your war, the Second World War. It was then that I discovered history was becoming more accurate. Academics were spending whole lifetimes studying the chronology of the Nazarene's life. I travelled to 2072 and found a definite date for his death, 7 April AD 30."

"Wow! What a story! What is the future like?"

"Don't go there! It's a world of outlaw bikers and

dusty plains. There is no order there, only chaos. I was killed, yet again, by vigilante vampire hunters; the usual thing, stake through the heart. But this time, they nailed me to the roof of a motel and left me to expire. They didn't count on the virgin on the bed loving me. Have you ever been crucified on a ceiling? Damned difficult to get down. I was dead but not *expired*. If you prepare by drinking the blood of a virgin, the body will die, but the spirit can still manipulate it for some hours. With Silvia's help, I was able to get down and find a new body. It's only the eleventh time I have been killed. I do hate killing the innocent … . Anyway, the future is full of Hot Boys and Hot Bullies."

"So we both fought in the same war!"

"Yes. Something else we have in common. Two soldiers lost in time!"

"Not so lost. Did you fight at Thermopylae?"

"No. But I was at Melos, so don't ask me about that massacre."

"Tell me more about your family."

"My father's name was Abreas, my grandfather's, Chariltheos. Now there is a name. Did you know 'theos' means 'God?' Until my grandfather's time, I was told, vampires lived like gods. Ach! But that is just the bedtime stories my mother told me."

"Can you tell me more about your form of time-travel?"

"I don't know you. The world is one, not of objects, but of *ideas*. I don't understand much more of it than that. But I can tell you that since our ancestors first lived on a diet of blood, they already had one foot in the next life. This makes it easier to move through time. But there is a price. Each time, one loses a little of oneself. A little spirit. A little hope. Evasion of death is even possible. But this brings a greater loss of hope. Our story is a sad one. There are many sad songs … ."

"But do you find you have to avoid making changes to events in the past?"

"Ah! The temporal paradox? It's a myth. I don't understand it, but events are not *set* by previous events. I have found that there is something, endlessly adjusting, changing things to stick to a plan. If you change something, they, or it, will adjust things, so that the events in the future occur exactly the same as if that *event* hadn't been changed."

"Hm. Interesting. So you are here to talk to Jesus?"

"Yes. If I can. That's where I am going tonight."

"But you know he won't speak to you? You think I wouldn't follow you if there was a chance?"

"I have to try. I'm going to sleep for a while before I go. That will be after sunset. You should rest too."

John settled back in the chair while I lay on my mattress. When I woke, I prepared to leave.

"Well. I won't wait up" John said.

"The Sweet Urn?" I asked as I put on a cape."

"Perhaps."

"Be careful. And if you're followed, don't bring them back here!"

***

I headed for the Garden of Gethsemane where Iesous would be, at the foot of the Mount of Olives, outside the City. I headed for the Gate of the Essenes, a small gate in the south west corner of the City and the only one open at night. It meant a long detour to get back round to the east of the city, so I walked fast. It would have been a small matter to change into a dog to move faster, but I had no wish to meet Christ naked.

As I searched for Iesous, I couldn't stop the feeling that my place was back at the inn. John's life seemed inextricably linked to Christ's in a way mine wasn't.

There was a brooding silence around the City.

Several men, with cloaks covering their faces, stood in the black shade of olives. Their heads seemed to follow my course as I wove through the grove. A man stepped in front of me, blocking my path.

"Where are you going brother?" he whispered.

"Oh. Nowhere. I was just walking. Why, is something happening?" I couldn't help my curiosity getting the better of me.

"Turn back brother or go another way." The glint of an eye under the full moon reflected his resolution. We faced each other tensely for a moment before I turned and retraced my steps. I circled round and tried again. I had gained more ground this time, but again I was stopped.

"Turn away!" another man told me. There was fear in his eyes.

This one has the sight. He knows what I am.

Few mortal men can know a vampire at first sight. I guessed he was close to Christ. I still wanted to continue.

"You will not be welcomed!" he whispered.

With a sigh, I retreated. It was not my intention to anger Iesous. I needed his blessing. Besides, the feeling that I should be with John was pulling me like gravity. And now I felt guilty about my final comment before leaving him. I returned to the inn.

"How did it go?" John asked. He was grinning. I pulled the stopper from the pot of wine. It was still half full. I moved close enough to smell John's breath.

"Have you been drinking?"

"I went out. To the first wine house I could find. To ask questions about The Sweet Urn.

"Idiot! Were you followed?"

"I don't think so. How about you? What did you find?"

"Nothing. Just as you said." I sat down. "And you?"

"Nothing. I don't even speak the language. I just about managed to order wine!"

"I can see you learned that skill quite well!"

"I'm going back to the Urn tonight. There's something there."

"I agree, but does it have to be tonight?" I was about to add that John should find a room of his own, but I held my tongue. Instead, I blurted, "Well then, I had better come with you. Let's go."

***

It didn't take long to reach The Sweet Urn. John was the only one to speak on the way there:

"It's pretty mad, going to the Urn on what is probably the most important night in Western history."

The Urn was buzzing now. It was packed to the doors with rich customers. We wore by far the poorest clothes, but once again, we were admitted. Apart from a few suspicious glances, we were left to our own conversation on a low table.

"I'm starving!" John declared. I didn't take him literally, but the fish and cake that were brought certainly made me feel a bit warmer toward the establishment. Fortunately, both our pockets were deeper than our kudras suggested.

We watched every dancing girl closely, but none were the tall one we had seen earlier. A shorter girl, with strong thighs and a very luscious body, caught *my* interest. She wore a diaphanous veil over her face and a light blue, long-sleeved kudra, brightly embroidered and decorated with beads. On her finger and ankles were tiny, silver bells. Even among the clang of plates and goblets, claps and the bellows of laughter I could still pick out the tinkling rhythm of her limbs as she swayed to the flute music.

I didn't expect to see her naked, but I was still

disappointed when she stripped to her sadin or undergarment. I gestured to one of the male attendants now circulating around the room.

"Can she reveal more?" I asked him. "At least her *face*." I implored.

"I shall ask her."

I saw her lean over to listen to his message from the side of the dance floor and utter something. He returned to me with her reply:

"Her face will cost you 30 shekels."

I handed him the money.

I was rewarded when the girl drew aside her veil at the end of the next dance.

Her brown eyes were complimented with high cheek bones, full, red lips and delicate ears pierced with gold pendant disk earrings.

"Egyptian," I suggested to John.

"I would hazard a guess, Thracian," he replied. I slapped my knee with delight. Not only did he have an opinion, but he might even have a point.

"Look!" John exclaimed.

The girl he had waited for had taken the dance floor. A slow, steady beat from a drum vibrated my goblet upon the table from somewhere.

"Do you feel it?" John asked.

"I feel better about this place than earlier," I assured him.

"No. The girl. I didn't tell you, I can sense evil. I can foresee doom. I have that feeling now."

"I didn't know what to make of John's words. I sat back to watch the tall girl dance. She was elegant, expressive and moved better than any girl I had ever seen.

"She must be a palace dancer who is just passing through," I told John. I have never seen her like before. She is far beyond our means or anyone in this room."

"Yes" John replied. He looked disturbed, rather than entranced. One of the attendants stooped to whisper in my ear:

"Would the Master like to meet the dancing girl in the blue kudra?"

"Yes."

While the tall girl still danced, the object of my fancy came and sat beside me on a cushion.

"What is your name?" I asked.

"Sarah."

"Eat!" I said, offering her a cake.

"Do you think they will let me see her face?" John asked me, indicating the tall girl.

"Ask," I replied. Sarah touched my wrist. "Speak," I told her.

"Don't ask about the tall girl," Sarah replied.

This was like a red rag to a bull for John.

He clicked his fingers at the nearest attendant, which made me wince.

"The girl dancing. Would she remove her veil?" I asked for him.

"She is not one of our dancers. She is only here to dance," he replied.

Even after all the dancers had all left the stage, and the candles were burning low, John still looked crestfallen. He only answered in monosyllables.

"I think we should be going," he suggested.

I peeled my lips from Sarah's and replied:

"Wait. At least this evening needn't be in vain for me. Sarah says she is retained by the Urn. But if I pay the house for her release, she can spend the night with me."

"And how much is the release?"

"Four minas."

"Four m-!"

John's indignant remark was cut short by a silk veil

brushing his cheek. The tall girl sat down beside him. After a moment to overcome his surprise, John said in Latin:

"Hello. What is your name?"

"You may call me … Ruth."

"You understand Latin!" John exclaimed.

"Ha! Yes, luckily for you."

Sarah's nibbling of my ear distracted me, but no girl ever introduced herself in these places, especially not in flawless Latin, so I listened intently.

"You are a fantastic dancer Ruth," John continued. "Are you from Jerusalem?"

"Ha! Ha! You interest me. I have been watching you."

Now I was gripped. I let go of Sarah and looked at John's partner. She released her veil to reveal a large, green emerald, hanging over her nose from gold circlet.

"You have? Why?" John replied. I was beginning to feel unaccountably sleepy. I suspected drugged wine, but when I tried to nudge John's elbow, I found that he was no longer beside me.

"Come!" Sarah whispered. "Pay the house."

My concern for my state of consciousness seemed outweighed by waves of euphoria. I managed to fumble in my purse for the money before being carried up the stairs to a private room. It was only there that I began to regain my faculties.

"It must have been the food!" I explained to Sarah.

She undressed demurely, and my fears allayed, I let her slowly undress me, while she kissed every newly revealed bit of my flesh.

"I love men with dark hair and beards!" she whispered. "You are *very* handsome."

"And you are very beautiful."

"There is something about you," she murmured. I rolled on top of her, kissed her two breasts delicately before easing apart her legs and entering her. The effect of the wine gave the world a rosy patina, and as we rose and fell together, I felt myself drifting away on the ecstasy of human intercourse.

"Time to go!" I announced after resting with her head upon my chest for a few minutes. Sarah didn't stir.

When I reached the ground floor, all but two candles were out in the main room. Only a little light, and one guard remained in the lobby.

"Has my friend left?" I asked.

"Still here," was the response. "Good night."

***

I waited under an awning opposite The Sweet Urn for John. When two burly men dragged him out and dumped him against a wall, hours later, I feared the worst.

"John? Can you speak? What happened? I am going to check your purse!" There was still nearly three minas there. That meant the Urn hadn't even charged him for his time with Ruth. Perhaps he had been too drunk to perform.

"Can you stand?" I asked.

John mumbled something, so I dragged him to his feet. Unsteadily, we began the long struggle back to the inn.

"I'm okay!" John declared after we had negotiated only a few blocks of the small city. "Wow! I don't know what just happened!

"Was she good?" I asked.

"Good? I feel incredible, but it's all a blur! I dunno. I was just out of it on something. I felt drugged. I feel that way now, a bit."

"I felt that too. But I was alright once we reached a room."

"Oh. Can we walk somewhere? I need a *lot* of fresh

air!”

“Probably a good idea. We’re being followed again!” I decided to lead John to Herod’s great Temple, in the east of the City. Dawn was just breaking, but it was a still day. If there was any breeze to be had, it would be upon the great Temple, in the Court of the Gentiles. It would also be busier there, less chance of attack.

“Who are they?” John whispered.

“I don’t know! You tell me! But they weren’t interested in me. I waited hours for you. Can you fight, if necessary?”

“Not yet. That Ruth; it was more like a dream than sex.”

“Probably the wine. Come on. Speed up a bit. They’re gaining.”

We passed the Theatre and turned left. I remembered the street being a wide one, but I was wrong. Ahead, a man in a white kudra stepped to block the narrow space.

I swung on my heels to check behind, and the two pursuers were only feet away.

“Draw!” was all I had time to tell John before my own drawn dagger parried a blow from the first sword.

“Take the one alone!” I gasped, leaping to the side to escape the second sword blade. They were quick, for humans.

I leaped again, this time for a flight of stone steps. I turned, just as the first attacker brought me within his range again. I allowed myself the indulgence of a little animal strength and speed. Parrying another determined blow, I flicked the blade away and brought my blade under his guard to strike at his heart. As I saw it penetrate, I saw that John was not doing so well. Both remaining attackers were striking at him. One of their blades caught his forearm and drew blood.

"I'm coming!" I yelled. In one bound I reached one of the two men and jabbed with my dagger, but to my surprise, he had already left the circumference of my swing. Both men backed away and ran into the main street.

"You certainly have a lot of friends in this city! Let me see your arm."

A slice of flesh, as long as my hand, had been torn away. John was holding the loose skin against his arm and grunting in agony.

"I never saw a man move so fast," he managed to say.

"They were after you again, not me. Why didn't you take your wolf-form?"

"It's not that easy. I can't do it just like that!"

"Nevertheless, you did well for an old man."

"I still feel groggy and *far too* old."

"Actually, your hair is a lot browner today than yesterday. You look about fifty. Help me with this body! We need to hide it. Where?"

I dragged the dead man's body further up the quiet street.

"Leave it!" John whispered. "They attacked *us*!"

"Nobody has seen us," I replied. "Here will do."

A narrow alleyway led between two houses to a courtyard. When I reached the courtyard, I bit into the dead man's neck. I sucked the gorgeous blood from the inert body, shuddering with guilty pleasure.

"I thought you said you didn't drink human blood!" John said from behind me.

"What I meant was that I never *kill* for human blood. I don't usually drink from veins; I prefer the arteries, but when needs must … . That's enough I think."

Tearing a strip of sleeve from the victim's kudra, I bound John's wound tightly.

"Let's go!" I whispered.

Returning to the main street, we turned left and soon after, arrived at the south west entrance to the great white building whose edifice rose far above us and dominated the whole of the City.

We ascended a long flight of steps, which turned ninety degrees to the right before reaching a tunnel that led into the Temple.

"I haven't been here for a while," I told John. "It's Passover today, so normally it would be packed with market traders, but it's almost deserted! Turn here."

I led John up some steps to the left and out into a giant courtyard, the Court of the Gentiles. I led John to the centre of the court where we sat on a balustrade.

"Just a faint breeze, but I feel better already," John remarked. "It's going to be hot today. No clouds. I wonder if the sky really will really become black tonight, as it says in the Bible?"

"Who knows? I never took it too literally."

"You were right. This place is deserted. Perhaps Jesus really did convince the traders to stay away. No wonder the Sanhedrin are scared of him."

"You mean the Sadducees. They control the Temple. Mind you, it's a warzone here for Jewish sects. They are all at each other's throats."

While we sat, watching the sun come up, a steady stream of Jews entered the Court. I turned to John:

"You should forget that bitch, Georgina."

"I can't. You may not understand, but she's just about all I have left.

"She has seduced you, virtually thrown you to the Serpents and kidnapped your wife. Creatures like me recognise the behaviour of demons."

"I notice you never call yourself a man, and yet

clearly you are one."

"Well, she sounds like a bitch to me."

John didn't answer me. He stared into space, and I left him alone for a while. I began to notice one word spoken frequently by those passing close by.

"Have you noticed something?" I asked John. "The Court is getting no fuller. All these Jews are going somewhere. My hearing is probably much sharper than yours. They are all talking about one person, Iesous."

We both spun round on the balustrade. We could see masses of people passing round Temple behind us and heading to the North side of the great Court.

"Let's go!" John suggested. "I don't know my Bible too well, but this is something we can't miss. Looks like we are finally in the right place at the right time."

We followed the masses to the north-western corner of the Court, where one of the two-storied pillared arcades that lined the edge of the great Court abutted the Antonia Fortress, a towering structure with four turrets at each corner.

The crowd was uneasy. It clearly consisted of several Jewish sects, and they were bellowing insults at each other. John and I pushed through to as near the front as we could get without being violent.

The crowd hushed.

From between the pillars we heard a voice announcing:

"Pontius Pilate is coming out to pronounce his verdict on Iesous of Nazareth."

I translated for John. I was bit taller than him too, and for an instant, I had a clear view through to the origin of the voice. A large chair sat under and awning. Two Roman Centurions stood to either side with their swords drawn. Fifty other soldiers lined the wall of the court beside them. A large man in a white toga came out and sat in the chair.

The Jews around me, most wealthy, jostled to hear what he was about to say. When he spoke, I thought his voice was rather weak for such a tall man. I only caught the first few words:

"I, Pontius Pilate … ."

"Not guilty!" exclaimed a man next to me. I had to shout to translate for John. The crowd erupted in protest. Both John and I raised our eyebrows.

The din went on for quite a while until somebody shouted something, and the crowd hushed. I asked a man next to me what was happening.

"Pilate is going to reconsider of course!" he replied curtly.

By the time Pontius Pilate's return was announced by one of the Centurions, my feet were aching from constantly trying to keep my balance in the chaotic crowd.

"Are you alright?" I asked John. "Perhaps we should leave." He looked pale, and his bandage was crimson with blood. Every few seconds he grimaced in pain as another body crashed into his arm.

"No. I *must* stay. It's just a few more minutes."

Again, Pontius Pilate spoke, but this time I could hear none of his words. I didn't need to. A great cheer went up from the Jews around me.

"Death! Death for the Nazarene!" they yelled.

"Condemned by his own people!" I yelled into John's ear.

"What did you say brother?" shouted a tall Jew, next to me.

I was ready to argue back, but John pulled my sleeve.

"Nothing!" I replied. "Come on John. Let's go." The Jew didn't understand my English but he understood that we were going to leave. He pushed me back.

"Don't push me!" I warned him, pushing him back.

"Another big man pushed his way through to me. I was about to push him too when he grabbed my assailant's sleeved and tugged the man back from me.

An ally!

In truth, I would have been better off without an ally. A scuffle broke out. Those against Iesous's verdict were few but enough to cause a disturbance. A trumpet blared somewhere, and most of the crowd began to back away from us. John was on the ground by this time, but only a few were left fighting around him. I pulled him to his feet just as a Roman soldier yanked at my sleeve.

"Come on John. Let's get out of here!" I yelled in English.

"No! Can't you see? This could be a chance … ."

John was dragged mercilessly away by two soldiers, and I was dragged after him.

***

Chapter Two

I hadn't quite understood what John's last words had meant, but as we were dragged lower into the Fortress's stinking bowels, I half expected to see the face of Iesous in every prisoner that grabbed the bars of his cage.

John was, by now, a limp body in the arms of the two guards ahead of me. I was relieved when we were both thrown in the same cell, a large one with about forty other tenants. The large man, who had fought beside me, was thrown in with us.

"We need water!" I yelled, as soon as the guards had left. "This man is hurt."

A crowd of curious prisoners parted, and a midget came through carrying a ladle of water.

The heat was almost unbearable in that cell. Most of the prisoners had stripped to their undergarments. Some had wrapped their kudras around their loins. John lay gasping for a few minutes before he gestured for me to pull him to his feet.

"How do you feel?" the midget asked John.

"Pretty crap actually. But thanks for the water. Is it normally this hospitable down here?" I think John was being sarcastic. The midget smiled but didn't answer.

There was a lot of noise, coughing and moaning, from other cells nearby, but our cell was silent.

I became aware that there was only one man, wearing the coarsest red kudra, in the dimly lit cell next to ours and began to think the unthinkable.

Could he be Jesus?

"John. John!" I whispered. "Look. Could it be him?"

"I don't know. He looks a lot like *you*! He looks pretty ordinary!"

"Just one man? In a cell as big as that? Praying like

that?"

John clambered to his feet, and we both leaned against the bars between the two cells, trying to get a look at Christ.

"Don't bother him," one of the prisoners said, touching me on the shoulder. He has only hours to live."

"Do you know who he is?" I asked, swinging round.

"They call him the Nazarene Rabbi. Some call him the Son of God. He has turned Jerusalem upside down, but his time has come."

I stared into the eyes of the man. Pride was gradually replaced by regret and then abject sadness. He shook his head. The other faces around him hung sadly above defeated shoulders.

"Can you try speaking with him?" John asked me. My lips felt dry. I swallowed nervously. It seemed the worst kind of intrusion to speak to this man. He was murmuring, deep in prayer, on his knees.

"Iesous!" I whispered. "Iesous!"

For a long time, he didn't reply, and I dared not repeat his name. I could only watch him.

"I hear you," he suddenly whispered in Hebrew. "I will come to you shortly. Be patient."

All sorts of thoughts sped through my mind while we waited. John seemed deep in thought. I didn't know what I was going to say.

"I don't have much time. I have much need of prayer," Christ said, when he rose and came to us. His eyes were fired by the most penetrating stare I have ever beheld. I truly felt naked.

"We understand Lord," John whispered. "We are both from the future and know your fate."

"No. You know the fate of my body. But you don't know how imperilled my soul is. I must be brief. I know of you John. Your friend, I know not, but I have heard of his kind. I have often wanted to meet one. You feel that you are not human and that God will not care for you."

I must admit, my eagerness overcame me, and I blurted:

"Yes! Yes! Please bless me."

"What have you done that is worthy of my blessing?"

"Nothin-…" Even as I spoke, I knew what I must do. A voice deep inside me echoed my own will: "You must do a good deed, something worthy of God!"

Iesous turned to John and held his gaze saying:

"You have a question for me."

I looked hard at Christ's face. Suddenly a smile flickered across it, and he appeared no more than an innocent and mischievous boy.

"Yes," John replied. "Where can I find the leader of the Serpents?"

"I am not concerned with the squabbling of Angels now, but I *can* tell you where to find the emerald-eyed horse from your dream. Everybody knows where to find the Merchant, Mentor. He owns the wine house in the Street of the Salt Sellers, near the Damascus Gate."

"Thank you. And can you tell me if it's possible to save Georgina?"

"Yes. If she is willing to do good, then it is possible for her to return to her own time. But she must fulfil her destiny."

John looked confused but Iesous continued:

"You must go now."

"But how do we get out?" John replied.

"Your powers will be more intense now. You will be able to bend these bars. I must pray."

Iesous turned away and began to pray. John gripped the bars and whispered:

"Wait."

I touched his shoulder.

"I could slip through these bars alone, but *you* need to do what he says," I said.

"But I don't know *how*!"

"Just try."

John gripped a bar at the front of our cell in each hand and seemed to struggle with himself for a long time. Then I heard a deep growl from his throat, like no sound I had ever heard from a man. He snarled once, and the bars began to bend. Loose stone dust fell on us from the bars' fixing points in the dungeon. John howled with the effort, and then he stopped. Both bars were bowed enough for him to slip through. I followed him and patted him on the back. He spun round and gripped my wrist so hard that I yelled.

"Your eyes!" I said, when I looked at him. They burned a deep red, tinged with yellow, like fire.

John let go of me and sped between the cells, back toward the stairs we had come down. I struggled to keep up!

Up the stone steps we sped until we reached an iron grill across the exit tunnel.

"Can you bend … ."

"Sh!"

John pushed me back against the wall. I heard a voice approaching the other side of the gate. We were concealed by a stone pillar, but as John squeezed himself further into the corner, I pressed against him.

The tinkling of keys in the lock was followed by a clang as the gate swung back. A burly man, whom I recognised as the gaoler, drew parallel to us. I grinned at him once before John leaped onto his back and wrenched his head to once side, breaking the man's neck. John took the ring of keys and a sword from the man and unlocked the gate. I followed him through, up some stairs and out into the bright sunlight. We were on a landing above the ramp that led to the Fortress.

"Cover your face!" I told John.

We walked quickly down the ramp, across the main road and into a maze of deeply shaded streets.

"Nobody followed us!" I declared.

"Amazingly," John added.

"Your arm!"

"What about it? Oh!"

John's bandage had slipped, revealing an arm without a wound. John touched it lightly before exclaiming:

"It's healed!"

"It must have been him!"

We headed toward my room as fast as we could without being conspicuous.

"You didn't seem as impressed with him as me!" I said.

"Probably, because I might be his descendent!"

"What? Well, you really are full of surprises!"

"Ha! But I don't understand why he mentioned *Angels*! What have Serpents to do with Angels?"

"I don't know."

***

When we reached my room, I gulped down some wine and food.

"Help yourself," I told John. I threw myself on the mattress. "I need to sleep and think about all this."

"Me too."

"I don't have a spare mattress. If I ask the landlord, there will be questions. Can you make do?"

"I didn't hear John's reply, because I was asleep.

"Wake up! Zosimyache! Wake up! We overslept!"

I was woken by John shaking my shoulder.

"What do you mean; we overslept?"

"Golgotha. Jesus Chris- ... . Sorry! Don't you know

your Bible?"

"Better than you know this Jerusalem! What time *is* it?"

"About two o'clock; early afternoon. Jesus will have been crucified by now. We should be *there*!"

"Why. Do you really want to see that man slowly dying?"

"Come on. Get dressed. I'm going, after I see this merchant's place. Where was it; the Street of the Salt Sellers?"

"Yes. It's on the way."

But we didn't get very far. At the first main street, we realised something was wrong. The street was empty of people. Two Roman soldiers stood either side of the end of the street. We dipped into a clothier's shop.

"What's going on?" I asked.

"Curfew. Sixteen prisoners escaped from the Antonia Fort. They are doing house to house searches. Of course, most people had already gone to that crucifixion, and now they have closed the Water Gate. Only the Essene gate is still open for those returning. I haven't seen one of them in here. Business is bad … ."

The man didn't seem about to stop opining, so we left.

"What now?" I asked John.

"Wait to dark, then we go; over the roofs if necessary."

"Your sword?" I suddenly remembered.

"Do you think it's safe?"

"No. But if we don't go soon, you might never see it again. Besides, my room is not safe. Somebody might talk."

We returned to my room but left again for the Upper Market within an hour. Above us, the sky was beginning to cloud over. I, too, was armed with a sword, concealed beneath my kudra.

Dodging from thin shadow to shadow and backtracking several times to go round Roman soldiers, we made it without incident to the Upper Market.

The armourer looked disappointed to see us but quickly covered this with a broad smile and then drew forth John's new sword.

"Indeed, a lovely piece of work," I told John.

We didn't have time for conversation. We set off for the Antonia Fortress, which was to the right of the street that led to the Damascus Gate.

We were aided by the fact that a great viaduct bisected the north and south side of the city at this point. It linked Herod's Palace to the great Temple, but there were few arches in the viaduct here, making this part of the City a kind of backwater. We saw no Roman soldiers until we reached the viaduct itself.

"Two guards, either side of the arch," I told John. Now they are walking past each other, crisscrossing. We won't get by now, unless you can change."

"I told you, it's not that *easy*. Even though I know what to do now, I am still too tired to try again unless it's strictly necessary."

"It's not."

What do we do then?"

"Wait. They change roughly every hour. The arch will be unguarded for a few of your minutes."

"When will that be? Do you have a watch?"

"I don't know and no. It doesn't matter. We wait."

***

We waited, hardly daring to breathe. After what seemed an eternity, I poked my head out from behind a balustrade and saw an empty arch, I waited a few seconds. No guards.

"Go!" I whispered. Within seconds we were through.

I turned to check where the fresh guards were.

"Plenty of time," I whispered, "But there's something else."

"What?"

"We're being followed again. Your friends."

"Oh great. Can you lose them?"

"Maybe. Easier if you take on wolf form."

"What, and arrive naked? And what about the sword?"

"Try it. You still had your clothes last time. We just need to move faster.

For a while it seemed as if nothing happened. Then John grabbed my shoulder and stopped. He stripped, picked up his sword and padded along beside me, his hands and feet slowly sprouting claws. Before long a muscular wolfman panted at my side. We picked up our pace, dodging through the shadows of the plusher apartments in Jerusalem but soon found ourselves in a cul-de-sac.

"We have to fight," I said. "It won't be hard. Better than dealing with them at the merchant's house. That would be embarrassing."

John answered with a growl, unnerving me.

"I see two entrances ahead. You take the left corner and I, the right. We'll ambush them."

But our pursuers were upon us before we were ready. We had to turn and fight in a tight space.

I leaped against the wall to one side of the five attackers. This brought me out behind them before they could even blink. Now, John and I could take advantage of the tight space and divide the five attackers at the same time.

Three turned to face me.

My blade flashed faster than they could respond. Two went down with cut throats. Well, there is no point prolonging things. The last was a swordsman of an entirely different order and managed to get past my guard and delivered a nasty slash to my back before getting away.

I elected not to follow him. I saw the first of John's parries and then the curved blade of the other swordsman flashed in the moonlight as it came down toward my friend's neck.

It took less than the blink of an eye for me to leap upon the man and deflect his blow. But in doing so, we both crashed into the wall, and he landed on top of me.

I watched, as if in slow-motion, while John struggled with *his* attacker. John's skill was by far the greater, but he held the sword in an unfamiliar paw. The enemy managed to get under John's guard and brought his blow round for a quick strike to John's heart. But John saw the move and spun away, rebounding off the wall. He managed to continue the spin and came around with a swinging strike to the man's neck.

My attacker tried to pin me down, and I lost sight of the other fight for a moment. I thought to draw my sword across his back, but before I could do it, he drew a dagger and sliced some muscle from my leg.

On impulse, I leaped back and to my feet. The man must have been surprised by my agility and strength, because he turned and ran.

I glanced at the other fight. John's blade must have missed, because the other man was still standing, although he was clutching his waist. Desperately, the man tried one last lunge, straight for John's chest, but my friend sidestepped and brought his blade against the other man's. John flicked the attacker's blade aside. With his forward momentum, the man passed John undefended.

"Now!" I said to myself.

John knew what he was doing. He calmly drove the blade between the man's ribs from behind. The attacker gasped once and skidded to a halt on the dirt.

I still heard the sound of blades engaging. I glanced past John and saw a man in a white crusader's tunic duelling with the first man that had escaped. Even more distinctive than the tunic was the second, huge sword that hung in a sheath on his right side. My second assailant joined the fray, but the knight was easily able to keep them at bay. After a few more strokes, one of the two attackers received a deep gash to the shoulder, and they both ran. The knight quickly followed them.

"Hey!" John growled, barely intelligible.

As I watched, my friend quickly returned to human form. I slapped him on his back, glad not to fear him.

"How did you *do* that?" I asked.

"I don't know! I just thought of what you said about the physical world being one of ideas. I thought of a wolf!"

"Let's get out of here!" I told John.

"Not until I find out more about who these guys are!"

John knelt over the dead body and felt for any concealed weapons or other items. Finding none, he ripped away the kudra from the man's arms and chest.

"Hm," he murmured.

"What is it?" I asked.

"Look. Strange."

I looked. There were rows of thin white scars up the man's arms, all the way from his wrist to his shoulder. There were also some on his chest and legs.

"Tribal markings?" I suggested.

"Maybe." John exposed the man's neck to me.

"Want some?"

"I'm alright for now. It doesn't seem like there is going to be a shortage if I stick with you. Come on, let's go!"

Holding my own leg, I led John to the end of the

alleyway and across a wide street. "Not far," I gasped.

"Wha- … ?"

"Not far. Are you alright?"

"Yes. You?"

"Twice wounded. The last time I was wounded was over a thousand years ago! You will be the death of me."

"One of us will die before this is all over."

"Great. Thanks for the confidence."

"Did you see that man?"

"Yes. Who is he?"

"I'm not sure. I think I know that face- … ."

"Where from?"

"Not sure."

"Come on."

Moments later we turned into a street that led to the main road outside the Antonia Fortress. I saw two soldiers at the end, but when we turned round, two others were just entering the street behind us.

"Up here!" I whispered. I climbed a row of steps to a first-floor landing and then used the branches of an old olive and a window to reach the roof.

"I'm *still* too old," John gasped when he reached the roof. "Now what."

"Along here," I said speeding along the flat roof toward the Fortress. Half way down the street, an alleyway broke our path. It wasn't wide for me, but I wasn't sure if John would make it.

"Don't stop!" I shouted.

I leaped over the gap and waited for John. He reached it, and with a look of angry concentration leaped into the air. Weighed down, as he was, by a long sword, the ten-foot gap was a lot to ask for.

John came crashing down on the very lip of the roof. His knee smashed into a tile, which dislodged and fell to the street. Nevertheless, his torso was far enough over the edge for me to haul him safely onto the roof.

"Fu- … !" he murmured, under his breath."

"You're alright. But the Romans will be onto us. Come on!"

Limping, John followed me to the end of the roof where we leaped to another landing and descended some stairs. We were past the Roman soldiers.

I led John across a wide street. The Antonia Fortress dominated the dark sky above us. My heart was in my mouth until we reached the cover of another street. We were now in the northern most part of the City and not far from the Street of Salt Sellers.

"Stop!" I whispered when I thought we were safe. "I need these bandaged. I am losing blood."

"Yes. Of course."

John bound my wounds expertly with his own undergarment, and we continued.

"The Street of Salt Sellers!" I announced.

We walked past closed shops and stone mason's yard, and there was the wine house on the left. I led John to the door. Above it, was a large plaque which read, in Hebrew, 'Municipal Wine House – open every festival week.'

"Good afternoon gentlemen," a doorman said. "Been out at the crucifixion, have we? You look like you *need* a drink!"

"Very funny!" John said.

"Well. At least this place is more friendly," I replied.

"Hm. I feel strange. This place *really does* make me feel weird."

"Not again. You and your feelings."

***

As we took our seats in a large courtyard, lined with olives and plants, I noticed that John seemed to be listening for something. I knew he wasn't smelling something.

"What is it?" I asked.

"Funny. I usually get very bad luck. But nothing bad has happened to me since I have been here. In fact, I have been luckier than *you*!"

"Great! Somebody who foresees doom and has bad luck. That's all I need!"

"Not doom, evil. But more of that in a moment. No, I mean, I really *do* have bad luck."

"Like what?"

"Well, for instance, that time I went back to the 13th Century. It started when I visited the British Museum in London. The reason doesn't matter, but I went to a telephone box to call my wife. I only had one coin left, and I dropped it. It bounced through a missing pane and rolled against a wall. I had to run after it, and I finally caught it against the wall. Knowing how these events usually end up, I glanced up. A window-cleaner's platform was crashing down on top of me. I just about got out of the way.

"Interesting."

"These sorts of things happen to me every week. Since I was a kid. But I can sense when they will happen. During the War, it saved my life many times and once, the whole of my crew in an aircraft. I was even interrogated over the phenomena."

"Wow! Alright, maybe you have something.

"What will you have, gentlemen?" asked an attendant. I translated for John.

"Oh. I will have red wine." John replied.

"Two red wines. And a glass of Egyptian beer," I said. "I ordered wine and a beer for me," I told John.

"Actually, I will have the beer too," John added. "And can I have a word with the owner, Mentor?"

"John!" I admonished.

The attendant raised both eyebrows at the name

Mentor thought he didn't understand the rest of John's request. I tried more tactfully:

"A beer too for my friend. Would it be possible to talk with the owner of this establishment?"

"Already sir? A complaint? But you haven't even been served yet?

"No. No complaint. I wish to speak with him on a business matter."

"The Master is not here now. I will convey your request when my master gets here."

"Does my blood show?" I asked John. I was in great pain and beginning to think of going back to the room at the inn, not that it was safe there either."

"You look fine. How do you feel?"

"As you say, like crap! But you said one of us will die. Is this one of your foresights?"

"Yes. I'm sorry, but I saw it. I just can't see who."

Now I wanted to go home, leave this place completely, but I *had* no home, anywhere.

I looked around the courtyard. It was almost empty. Only a few rich Jews were there, perhaps those able to bribe the Romans. The wine and beer arrived. John was eager to try the Egyptian beer.

"Mm. Warm, as beer should be but very sweet."

"It's sweetened with honey."

"Mm. Not exactly Newcastle Brown but *I like* it!"

He sat back in his seat.

"You know," he said. "I have been thinking, I think maybe I know what those marks were on that man."

"Well?"

"You know I mentioned the Concilium Putus Visum, the CPV?"

"The Catholic assassins?"

"Yes. They always sign letters, usually veiled threats, in their own blood. That means they have to cut themselves quite deeply. Do you follow my thinking?"

"Yes. But those two swordsmen that got away. They were in a different league. They were swordsmen, the like of which I have rarely seen. And they were using Samurai blades, if I am not mistaken."

"Yes. I noticed. I don't understand that. The CPV usually use garrottes, so I wasn't surprised they were only average with a sword. The first ones, I mean. Hm. I don't know. There's something else I haven't told you."

"Go on. I'm not going to die just yet."

"I am from an order called Ordo Lupus."

"Brotherhood of the Wolf? No surprises there."

"Well, it *was* for me. It turns out that every other generation of eldest boys in my family has been a werewolf, so far as I can tell, for thousands of years. My grandfather was one, and I think he wanted to tell me that, but something prevented him. He died in mysterious circumstances, and his grave was a fake. His body wasn't there. He wanted me to know that. My parents tried to cover a lot of this up. I found out what I really was by accident. And with a little help from Herleva. I used to think of us as Wolf-Angels. But let's face it. What I really am is a werewolf, plain and simple."

"Not plain."

"Ha! No, I guess not. Anyway, what was I saying? Oh yes, well what I wanted to tell you is that the CPV serve the Catholic Church. At first, they were protecting me, but then they wanted to punish me. But they never tried to kill me. Now they seem intent on my death, just at a time when I think I am doing something which cannot possibly harm the Church. It doesn't make sense. Something is wrong. Something has changed."

"A lot seems wrong here. And beware of that merchant. Most wine houses are only open for the Thursday, Friday and Saturday of the Festivals. Only the downmarket wine houses stay open for the whole of the three Festival weeks, Monday to Sunday, as this one does. But this is the best of them and does the best trade. It's the only one that has 'Municipal' above the door. That means the owner has done some deal with the Roman authorities. Mentor must be a powerful man.

"Yes, he is a powerful man and a dangerous one!" a bejewelled Jew said, leaning toward us. I heard you asking the attendant for him. I have seen him, wearing that green emerald of his between his eyes. That's why some call this the Third Eye. But he's a strange man. Some say he is a magician. I haven't seen him for nearly a week."

"Thanks for the warning," I replied. I translated his comments for John.

"That's the kind of man I am looking for. Why are the festivals always on a Friday?"

"Yes, I wondered about that. Because the Jews follow a solar calendar. Causes a lot of friction with the Romans."

"You've finished your beer. Another?"

"Please. Helps with the pain."

"Another thing I don't understand," John continued. "Why on earth was it a horse in my dream?"

"I don't know. Tell me more about this aging thing and how long you and this girl have."

"Well, we each get younger by nineteen years, every day. That's what I was told. Georgina would have been about thirty in the year 1995, which is *when* she came from. I was seventy in 2000, which is *when I* came from. I am guessing here, but it seems to me she has under one day before she reaches an age of sixteen, the same as me. Apparently, any younger than sixteen, and the heart and mind cannot take the strain any more. That's about it!"

"Well, you *do look* about thirty now," I told John.

"Your hair is completely brown."

***

Several times, I asked the attendant if the Mentor had arrived, but it was only well after the middle of the afternoon that he smiled when we saw him.

"My master is here gentlemen. What is more, my master will see you in a short while. A drink on the house?

John was, by this time, more than eager to leave for Golgotha.

"The owner is here," I told John. "He will see is in a few minutes, and they are bringing us complimentary wine."

"Fine. I hope he hurries."

"Rich men rarely hurry."

After finishing the drinks, quickly, we were ushered to a plush apartment on the second floor. We were both invited to sit on silk cushions, and then the attendant left us.

Moments later, from behind a bead screen, stepped a tall figure who said:

"Greetings."

It was none other than the tall girl we had seen in The Sweet Urn! She was veiled and hooded in black and stayed out of the candlelight. But there was no mistaking her height and feminine voice. She sat, cross-legged, opposite us.

"Ruth?" John asked in Latin.

"Yes. You may still call me that."

"But what are you doing here!"

"I have taken over the place. I own it now," she replied.

John and I both looked at each other.

"Forgive me," I interjected, "but you are a woman! How is it possible?"

"Anything is possible," she replied and then quickly added, "With money."

"Err, I am still recovering from the other night," John began. "Either you slipped me a Mickey Finn, or else you are the best lover on Earth!"

"Ha! Probably the latter. But what's a Micky Finn?"

"Never mind?"

"You are probably wondering why I would dance in that club and then spend the night with you?"

"Err. Yes!"

"As I have told you, I was curious about you. Now what can I do for you?"

John must have been a bit put off by her coolness, because it took him a moment to recover, so that he could ask his question. Besides, it was about another woman, so I didn't envy him.

Ruth started unwinding her veil and let it slip to her shoulders. Between her beautiful green eyes was the same, huge emerald we had seen before. She smiled at our evident curiosity.

"Mentor wore it too," she said. "I wear it, so that some might not be aware he has left. They actually think I am him, if I cover everything but my eyes and don't walk. He was a vain man and of similar height."

"Do you know anything about a woman called Georgina?" John asked. I winced.

"Hm. I am tired. It's been nice seeing you again John, but I think this discussion is at an end. One of my men will show you out."

She rang a tiny bell and stepped back through the bead curtain.

"Wait!" John said.

"Don't go to the crucifixion!" the feminine voice said from behind the curtain. The door behind us opened.

"This way gentlemen," the man told us.

"She definitely knows something about Georgina!" John whispered, as we walked away from the wine house.

"But she's not going to say it," I added.

"I still don't understand why it's a *horse* in my dream!" John hissed.

Above us, thickening black clouds were beginning to swirl in a great vortex.

"I have seen this before," John told me.

"What does it mean? It's as dark as night!"

"It means bad things are gonna happen! I expected it to get dark. The Bible says so. But I have never seen it on *this* scale!"

***

"Which way to the Essenes Gate?" John asked me.

I led him cautiously through back streets to the south-western corner of the Lower City. We were expecting to see the Gate surrounded by Roman soldiers, and that's what we found.

"No way through there!" I whispered from our vantage point in the porch of a closed shop. "Let's go back. This is pointless."

"No. I *have* to see him."

A few tired Jews, mostly poor, wandered into the City through the Gate.

"Go straight to your houses," a Roman Centurion bellowed after them.

"Alright then," I said. "I have an idea. Follow me."

I led him back to the Street of the Salt Sellers. We walked brazenly along the streets. Twice we were challenged by Roman soldiers. Twice, I replied:

"We are returning from the crucifixion." We were waved on.

"What are we doing here?" John asked, when we reached the stone mason's yard.

"You be a look-out for a few minutes."

It wasn't too difficult to snap the crude bolt in the lock to a workshop by wrenching the door free from the frame. I liberated two of the longest lengths of rope I guessed would be there.

"Wrap this around your waist under the kudra" I told John. I saw that John was wearing a money-belt under his kudra, not dissimilar to my own, but his had a pocket, containing a small, black book.

"What's that?" I asked, pointing to it.

"My journal. It's a bad habit. I keep one all the time."

We set off for the south wall of the City.

"Roughly at the end of this street is a bastion, on the other side of the wall. It's about two hundred feet from the nearest tower, to the left. They will never see us once we get over the top," I explained.

"Over what?"

"We reached the end of the north-south road where it was crossed at right angles by another. On the opposite side towered the South Wall of Jerusalem. Rows of huge limestone blocks towered to heights of fifty feet in the walls around the City.

"We're going up *that*!" whispered John.

"How tall do you think it is?" I asked.

"Shit! About thirty-five feet, I would guess."

"Listen, tie a piece of your kudra to the end of this," I instructed, unwinding my rope and tying a single loop around my waist. "No point in us both being out there. When I tug it a twice, come up. Can you climb it?"

"I don't know. My arms still ache from the fight. I'm not a young man yet. I am still about thirty, remember?"

"Alright. I'll pull you up."

"But how will you get up?"

I didn't wait to explain. I sped across the wide-open space and reached the wall. Leaving the rope coiled on the ground, I concentrated on the agility of a bat and began climbing the large blocks effortlessly. Two Roman soldiers were approaching along the road.

I cast-the-cloak and effectively became invisible to the soldiers. Humans are easily distracted. If anybody had seen me, they would have only seen a shifting shadow for the blink of an eye.

I climbed on, and I could hear two more soldiers talking on the wall-walk above. Near the parapet, I waited until they had gone. I clambered onto the wall-walk and peered over the wall. With my keen eyesight, I could see that a few coils of rope lay on the ground. I hauled these up until the end dangled above the ground and yanked it twice. Within a few seconds, I felt the heavy weight of John on the rope, and I began to pull. John finally clambered over the edge and stood beside me, gasping.

"What … now?" he whispered.

"I lower you down and then follow you," I replied.

As I had guessed, about thirty of your feet further along the wall was the bastion, jutting out from the city. It only protruded about ten feet, but it formed two angles with the wall, and the nearest angle was obscured from the tower where guards peered out into the night. More importantly, the angle's shadow hid us from the citizens returning from the crucifixion. Any one of them might turn us in for a few shekels.

Within a few more minutes, I had lowered John, struggling, to the ground, dropped the rope and followed him.

"We don't need the other rope," I said. "Let's go.

"Red wine! White wine! Two shekels per log! Sixteen shekels per hin!" croaked an old man, as a younger man handed out the wine from a wagon.

"Disgusting!" John murmured.

"Stop!" I told him as he veered toward them.

It didn't take us much longer to reach the first coil of citizens looped around the three dying men on crosses.

There was no hill, no golden light, not even profound murmurs from any of those crucified. There was only the heartrending moans of pain from the dying men.

Still, the spectators were transfixed. Many of them had eyes opened to their limits. Other's faces were downcast and mournful. Some even looked guilty. None wanted to stop watching.

"There's nothing for us here," I whispered, catching John's sleeve.

"No. Nothing!" John replied. "I, I don't want to look. Wait!"

"What?"

"What's that? Do you see it?"

"Where?" John was pointing to a patch of dirt on the other side of the crosses.

"I see nothing!"

"The air. It shimmers. I've seen it before; it's a Serpent. It's watching."

John seemed to slip into a trance. I shook his shoulder, and he murmured:

> "Iam non est tempus,
> Cras erit vobis.
> Ego autem sum Necrotari,
> Impatiens sum, mi Amice."

"What's that? Come on! Let's get out of this place. I don't like it!"

"Sorry. I don't know what happened! Yes, let's go!"

But before we could get very far, a man in a blue turban stepped in front of us. This caught my attention, because it was the first turban I had seen in Jerusalem.

"Are you leaving already?" the man asked. "Let me introduce myself. You may call me Mara bar Serapion[1]."

"We're not staying," I replied. "Please let us pass." John simply stared at the man. I felt that the situation was rapidly getting beyond my control.

"I make a pilgrimage here every year, on my Birthday," the man continued.

"To Jerusalem?" John asked.

"No. To Golgotha, as you call it, to watch this!"

He swept his hand across the scene behind us.

"Let's go," I pleaded with John.

I steered him quickly between the olives and back to the wall. I found it much easier to climb. Once over, we darted from shadow to shadow, on the way back to my room.

"Your wounds!" John exclaimed. You're moving really easily again!"

I undid my bandages.

"You're right!" I replied. "I never thought he would heal *me*."

"See, you *are* human," John declared. "Did you hear what that man said?" He whispered. "He comes back every year! He must be a time-traveller too!"

"Mad, more likely."

"I'm not so sure. There was an atmosphere around him. Did you feel it?"

"No. You say that about almost everyone."

"No. I mean it. Don't you ever feel that everything around you is less than solid? That you are the only solid thing?"

"Hm. Now that you mention, I have felt that

once or twice. As if everything else is fading dream. I put it down to the number of years I have travelled and the amount of time-travel I have done."

"But didn't you feel it as a child?"

"I don't know. Come on." The thought made me uncomfortable.

"That man; what was his name?"

"Mara bar Serapsomething."

"Serapion. He felt more real than me!"

"Like the Serpents?"

"No. They seem less real, more like an illusion."

"Hm. And that prayer? Or whatever it was you were muttering?" John translated from Latin to English:

"Now is not your time,
Tomorrow you will see.
But I am Necrotari,
I'm impatient for you, my friend."

"Great! Somebody else wanting you dead!" I said.

"Not wanting. Expecting. Still doesn't mean you're safe though!"

"Thanks."

***

We reached the courtyard, behind the inn, but I held John back.

"Wait!" I whispered.

I crept forward. I could see the marks of many boots, some hobnailed, in the dirt. They had obliterated our own tracks and those of the normal courtyard inhabitants, goats.

Indicating that John should stay put, I drew my sword and climbed the steps. I leaped into the room, turning about to look for intruders. There were none, but the room's contents were all damaged, wine pots, clothes, cushions, chairs and the table. Even the mattresses had been slashed.

"Let's go!" I told John when I returned to him. "It's not safe here anymore. Roman soldiers, possibly informed by your friends, the CPV. Possibly they came too. Somebody has been looking for something. Everything has been ripped apart."

The curfew was lifted an hour later, more, we thought, because of protests from the traders than, because the Romans had found the prisoners. But then again, perhaps they now knew enough. We had found another room in the Lower City by this time. It was not ideal. There were two routes out of the inn courtyard, but the room was at the front, small and fly-ridden. At least the proprietor was half-blind.

John rested until he heard the crier announcing the end of the curfew. I had fallen asleep. When I woke, I lay, watching two flies preening themselves on the loaf of bread, for some time.

I can't believe he healed me! Perhaps I am human after all?

"What now?" I asked over some of the bread, stale cheese and more wine.

"He's already dead. It's early evening," John replied. After sighing, he announced, "I have to see where Ruth goes. She is up to something. It's okay. I can go alone."

"Are you joking? He healed me! And I haven't even done much yet. I want to do some great deed of good, even if it's just to see what happens. I am coming with you. Put on the kudra I bought last night. You won't get anywhere with one blue and one brown. There will be a reward out for such a man."

John and I both dressed in the nomad versions of kudras, which I had purchased. They had a scarf which, shielded the eyes from the sun by casting them into shadow.

We left for the area of the Third Eye, once belonging to the merchant, Mentor, and now belonging to Ruth.

It was unusually cool, even for April, and as dark as any midnight. Jerusalem's citizens were terrified of the unnatural darkness, and many muttered that they were all cursed. An old man wandered past us, croaking:

"The Nazarene is dead! We have all sinned!"

I glanced behind me, as I do habitually, and caught the glint of reflected candle light on a sword.

"You'll never believe this," I announced. "but we're being followed again."

As we wove though the twisting turns of the Lower City, our pursuers drew closer and became bolder. When we turned into a quieter street, it looked like combat was inevitable. But I turned round and they had vanished.

A street later, I understood why.

"Seems like the knight scared them off," I told John.

"You know I told you I thought I knew that face? Well, I couldn't be sure in the dark, but now I am. I want to speak with him."

"He doesn't look like he wants to speak to us. I have an idea. At the next turn, keep walking ahead beside that man in a black kudra. Keep going in a straight line, or I will lose you."

At the turning, John did as I asked, and I turned left. I ran to the end of the block and took another left, then another, until I came back onto the road where I left John. Sure enough. I could see the mysterious man, trying to hide behind a cart, drawn by a donkey. I crept up behind him and grabbed both his arms.

"Let go of me!" he yelled in English. He was

surprisingly strong for such an old man, but I was far stronger.

"Come with me," I told him. "There is somebody who wishes to speak with you."

At the next street corner, we caught up with John, who was somewhat surprised to see us. He even raised both eyebrows at the knight.

"Into this porch," I told them both. I dragged the knight into the porch of a closed basket shop, and John followed. John pulled down the blue-eyed man's hood and stared at a red birthmark under the knight's left ear.

"It *is* you! Grandad!"

"John! I often wondered if I would meet you here!"

"So why have you been hiding from me?"

"Hiding? I only saw you last week. You came out to my house!"

"Eh? Oh. No, I mean here! You have been following me but keeping out of sight."

"I wasn't sure that it was you! I have never seen you as an old man! But there's no time! I know why you're here, and that's why I'm here! The big fight is coming. I was sent ahead to find you. Now I have to get the others!"

"Others?"

"Ordo Lupus. Some of us can use the Gates, although you are the best. You are the most talented of our Order for a thousand years. I have to find those that are willing and able and bring them here. I can maybe find half a dozen or so. Have you found her yet?"

"Georgina?"

"Yes."

"No."

"Oh. Well you will. You must! I have to go back *now*. All my life has been for this. I cannot fail!"

"But how will you get back. There *is* no way back from here. That's what I was told."

"There is! A Gate; on the Mount of Olives. Don't ask me who put it there. I only discovered a reference to it by accident. It was only a guess until I found it. It's half way between an olive with no leaves and a stone tomb. This one stays open for longer than any other; the beam shines at noon for three days either side of the full moon, but it works the same way. Whoever makes these Gates cannot be far from here."

John grabbed his grandfather's arms and, in doing so, pushed aside the cape the old man had draped over his medieval tunic. The huge sword was revealed.

"Is that it? The Sword?" John asked.

"The very same. You wielded it I believe."

"I thought it was destroyed."

"It will be, by you."

"Does that mean that the Serpent is here too?"

"Chalcathgna? The one you will defeat? Yes, he's here and many other Serpents. I have to go. Where will I be able to find you?"

"I have to watch Ruth. You know her?"

"No."

"On the south side of the Third Eye courtyard; I will leave a message."

"Good. Keep going my boy. You are doing wonderfully."

"But you never taught me *anything* about Ordo Lupus!" John yelled after him as he left the porch. My friend sounded angry.

"I never needed to!" the old man replied as he turned the street corner.

***

I didn't have to lead John back to the Third Eye. He knew the way. There were two entrances to the Third Eye, the main one, into the public courtyard and a rear one, through a narrow courtyard at the bottom of a long flight of steps. John stationed me at the front while he took the rear. We could both see each other from our concealed positions.

"If you see her, don't do anything stupid!" I told him. "And signal me if you are going anywhere."

We waited until well after the middle of the night. I felt myself falling asleep and jerking awake several times. At last, the last patrons and attendants left the Third eye. This made me more alert. But after another hour and no sign of Ruth, I was again on the edge of sleep.

Falling asleep wouldn't have been so bad, if it hadn't been for the mass hysteria that had taken over the City. This meant that nearly every one in ten passers-by was a nervous Roman soldier. Even if they hadn't recognised us in our nomad attire, they would surely arrest us for suspicious behaviour.

"We have to go," I whispered to John, who had only jerked awake when I touched his shoulder.

"You're right. I can't stay awake any longer."

We slept until well after what would have been daybreak, but of course it was still dark. John seemed particularly agitated when we shared what was left of the food.

"Listen," he blurted. "I'm not the sort of guy to rush into a fight with the odds stacked against me. I don't mind *risk* but I want a *chance*. If what my grandfather tells me is true, I cannot hope to liberate Georgina on my own. Against *all* the Serpents, I would be next to useless. There are said to be twelve of them, and they are *awesome*!"

"There's that number again; twelve."

"I have seen one kill a row of knights in less than a blink of an eye. Even if my grandfather does gets back with six Ordo Lupus members, werewolves, it won't be nearly enough. I may as well give up now! How long would it take you to get some of your friends here? You don't need the Gates, do you?

"Are you *mad*? First of all, what friends? I don't have any … *vampire* friends. I think you have a very great misconception about *vampire* life! It's not a world of happy friends, all going around drinking the blood of victims as if it were ice cream! Secondly, if I did have any *friends*, none of them would have the slightest reason to get involved in *this*! Thirdly, you need me … for *protection*. Are you sure this is not more that you resent my help and want to get rid of me?"

John took longer than I would have liked to answer.

"We are weak in numbers. I have to save Georgina for personal reasons. I can't let her go. But more to the point, Christ seems to think she is important in some way. That's it. Those are my reasons. You have only known me a day. When I saw you leaning over me, I knew there was something … strange about you. At first, I thought you were a Serpent. You 'feel' similar. I have no doubt you have been to dark places. But you've been a good friend so far." John took a deep breath. "I don't know where this is heading, probably to my death, maybe to yours, but I *need* you."

"Well, quite a speech! How can I refuse? There is one person who could help. However, the last time I saw him, he was hell-bent on his own self-destruction. It would take me a few hours to get back here. Unfortunately, *I* cannot return before I left, as you seem to be able to do with your Gates.

"Ha! That might be possible, but I have been warned not to try. For sanity reasons."

"You want me to go now?" I must have sounded hurt, because John smiled warmly and then laughed. He looked like a naughty boy.

"Yes. If you can. I can manage on my own for a few hours. It's just a case of waiting."

"You know this is all probably a trap, don't you?"

"It could be, but what choice do I have."

"Well, don't do anything stupid. Right then. Do I have everything? See you later."

Leaving the inn, I bought a spectacular gold necklace with my remaining shekels and headed out of the City. I would need to run to escape 1st Century Jerusalem, and it was better not to be seen.

***

When I emerged from the veil, I was in a familiar courtyard of Paris in the summer of 1794. I came to a halt and fell to my knees on cobble stones.

Out of the frying pan and into the fire!

I was in the midst of a revolution, and I had to find somebody who *wanted* to get himself executed!

Claude will either be in his garret or one of the coffee houses.

It was night here too. A nightingale's sweet song was interrupted by the crunch of coach wheels on grit and the cough of a prostitute or her patron.

I headed straight for Claude's fifth storey room in the Rue des Dechargeurs, where I could change into something appropriate.

Only two blocks away from Claude's room, I passed the notorious Cemetery of the Innocents, a squalid tangle of graves, the bodies of which often surfaced in the streets or cellars of nearby buildings.

I found Claude's key in its usual hiding place and let myself in. I quickly changed into a waistcoat, pantaloons and overcoat and set of for one of nearby markets. There was a distinct air of disuse about the room. A few red grapes on a place already had a fine fur on them.

Not good.

I found the coffee house I was looking for and went

straight up to the patron.

"Gaston. Have you seen Claude?"

"Monsieur Antoine! How good to see you. You seem to have grown a rather large beard and moustache in two days! Perhaps you are now an actor! A nice glass of cognac for you?"

"No. Just the location of Claude. I don't have much time."

"But surely you have heard? I mean, I don't know if it's true, but I heard he has been arrested and taken to the Bastille!"

"Oh no!"

"You know what he's like. He accosted two gentlemen here yesterday. He was shouting all sorts of obscenities about the Revolution to them. I have a feeling one of them reported him!"

"Gaston. I need money. What I have in my pocket is worth at least a 4 louis. It's a genuine gold necklace from 1st Century Jerusalem. You can have it for all the money you have in the house now. That leaves you with what you take for the rest of tonight. I promise you will make a pretty profit. Have I ever lied to you?"

"No! Perhaps it will please my wife. Let me see it!"

After haggling, Gaston handed over the money. Even he knew he had a bargain at the price of half his takings. He would sell it for twice that the next day if he wished.

"Thank you, Gaston! Hopefully, I will see you very soon, with Claude!"

Claude! I only left you two days ago, in your time. How could this happen so soon! Only one thing is going to get me into the Bastille! Money!

But at his flat, I found none. When I reached the Bastille, I had already counted what I had in my pocket; twenty-five livres. I knocked on the wooden gate.

"I'm here to see a prisoner!" I announced.

***

In Paris time, this had taken me about two hours. Two hours after I left John, he was still watching the Third Eye. I know what happened next, because I read it later in his journal. Why I was reading, I will explain later. This is what I read:

I waited for one hour after Zosimyache left before resuming my watch on Ruth's back door. The sky was still as dark as night. But after only an hour, I saw a tall figure leave, fully concealed in a black kudra and head scarf. There was no doubt this was Ruth. The figure had the easy hip swing of a mature and confident woman. I took extreme care to stay out of sight.

"This is one sharp woman," I told myself. I was fortunate that the streets were fairly empty, so I could still see her from quite a distance. She didn't seem to fear being followed and walked past the Fortress, under the viaduct and on to the top part of the Lower City.

Here she turned right and then into the first house on the left. It was a nondescript and run-down house. I waited for about a minute and then casually walked past the house. I reached a trelliswork in the front courtyard of the next house. Through the pink flowers' stems which climbed up the trellis, I could see into the rear courtyard of the run-down house. But there was nothing to see. I waited nearly three hours before returning to Zosimyache's room. I was sure my friend would have returned and that he could stand guard while I grabbed a few hours' sleep. But when I reached the room, the wooden door, which we had locked, was hanging off its hinges. I froze.

"They must be watching me," I told myself. "Now what? Check the room, quickly!"

There was no blood or any other sign of a struggle. I ducked my head back out of the room and set off for the nearest busy market in the Lower City. Three men in white followed me. I would try to lose them.

I found myself humming Tomb Thumb's Theme again! Funny how one reverts to childhood when stressed!

They were still tailing me when I left the market. It was time for a different approach.

I turned into a busy street and found what I had been seeking, a long flight of steps, near the corner. I recalled the few minutes with Jesus and what I had learned. Focusing on the deep anger that ran like a black river through my soul, I willed my lupine muscles to grow but restrained myself from a full transformation. My huge thigh muscles tensed and then I leaped down upon my two pursuers.

I hoped the very public place would make them run, but they chose to fight.

"I have had enough of you!" I growled. All three men sprang back at the monstrous sound of my voice. My blade flashed through the night. In a moment, I had sliced through the two men with samurai swords. The lesser warrior, behind them, turned to run.

"Sorry. Today's not your day," I muttered before driving the sword clean through his heart. "That's what I think of the CPV!"

"Monster from Hell! Return whence you came!" yelled a voice behind me. I spun round faster than I thought possible.

A bullet from a pistol was half way to my chest. With a skill I had only dreamed of, I brought my blade up to deflect the bullet. The loud 'clang' of impact was followed by a 'zip' as the bullet missed my ear by less than an inch.

More bullets were coming my way. The man with the gun was still pulling back the trigger as fast as he could. I dodged three bullets. The last two were too close to miss! I twisted like a supernatural dancer to move my hip out of the way, but one bullet went straight through my flesh, just above the bone. The second bullet slashed a deep wound in my free arm. But I was still standing.

"Pastor Michel! A pleasure! I gasped.

"Monster!" he said once more. "Werewolf!" He bellowed at the top of his voice. It was too much. I leaped toward his turning body and sliced him almost in two, from the shoulder to the hip. His distorted body flopped on the ground.

I had to resist an animal howl of triumph, before loping off toward the viaduct. Onlookers were screaming in terror at the scene of the massacre.

When I lost the rage, my two wounds began to slow me down, but I was already near the house Ruth had entered. I was leaving a trail of red dots in the grit behind me. I would probably die from infection, but I just needed to stay alive for one more day. I found climbed into the garden of an empty house and applied tourniquets to both wounds.

I was terribly thirsty as I took up my vigil again. It was early afternoon, and if it hadn't been black as night, I couldn't have borne it.

Six hours later, I could bear the pain and thirst no more. I stood up to leave and stopped, stock-still.

The tall figure wearing the black kudra was again approaching the house. I ducked down behind the wall that concealed me.

Ruth entered the house and emerged into the rear courtyard. She glanced left, right and behind her and walked to a small outhouse with a faded, blue door. She took something from her sleeve, opened the door and disappeared inside the outhouse.

Of course, my interest, and endurance was restored by this event. I had hardly even noticed the outhouse, the first time. Now I stared intently at that door.

"Is Georgina inside?"

The thought was mouth-watering.

A passer-by sold me his gourd of wine and some bread for an extortionate amount but I resolved to wait a while longer. As the air cooled even more, I checked my wounds. The bleeding had eased, and I was getting used to the pain. Besides, I was now a lot younger and fitter. I waited and watched. But when another passer-by told me it was already past midnight, I grew desperate.

"I'm going in!" I told myself.

There had been plenty of time to plan my next move. Before I entered the outhouse, I needed to pass on the intelligence to my grandfather and Zosimyache. I was perplexed at my friend's non-appearance, but I *knew* he would come back. However, it was going to be difficult to contact both of my allies. Only one method had occurred to me. I stumbled to the Third Eye, still whistling Tom Thumb's Theme, and searched in the dusty gutters, further along the Street of the Salt Sellers. I saw him; a street urchin who was desperate enough for a shekel to risk his life and spoke a little Latin.

"Wait here. It could be days. When you see either an old man with a white beard and a red cross on his tunic or a nomad in a black kudra and scarf go to the gate of the Third Eye, stop them before they reach it and tell this this; third street on the right, past the viaduct and first house on the left. Outhouse at the rear. Do you know the Third Eye?

"Yes master."

"Repeat the message."

After he had learned the message correctly, I told him:

"Don't tell anyone what I told you, or you will be killed. And I want you to tell both men. They may come together or at different times. Here is a shekel now. If you do everything correctly, there will be a second shekel for you."

With my message left, it was time to go. Minutes later, I climbed over the wall to the courtyard of the run-down house. I crept to the outhouse and tried the door.

"Locked! An iron pin tumbler too!"

Once again, my animal anger came to my aid. Grunting with the effort, I broke the lock away from the wooden door and peered inside. A faint glow lit a crude set of steps in the dusty floor. I closed the door and stumbled down the steps.

***

Chapter Three

In Paris, I was admitted to the Bastille only after paying the gate keeper a sizeable bribe. Down dingy, fetid corridors he led me and down steps to a subterranean row of cells.

"Stand well back from the door. If you touch the prisoner, I have orders to shoot. Five minutes."

The filthy guard withdrew to a discrete distance and withdrew an apple from his pocket. Polishing it on his sleeve, he took a showy bite from the fruit and grinned at me.

"Fifteen minutes?" I asked.

"A livre goes a long way for a prison guard."

I tossed him the coin and looked at the grate in the cell door. It was empty of any face.

"Claude!" I called out. "Claude!"

"Go away!"

"It's me. Morell!"

"Morell?" Claude's face appeared. "You said you would never come back!"

"What are you doing here you idiot. Do you know what they do with agitators these days?"

"That's what I want. It's alright for you. You are older, you remember good times, and every woman you meet seems to fall for you. I am sick of killing, drinking blood, stalking people, paying for a woman, drinking her blood and then having to run. Or live in filth like my current … last … place!"

Claude had already lowered his voice to a whisper, so much that only I could hear it. Even if a prisoner in the next cell could hear us, my life too would be in danger. I whispered back:

"I only have fifteen minutes. Listen Claude, I have met somebody. Do you remember I told you that I wanted to meet Christ? Well I did. But the man who led me to him is special too. He's a werewolf!"

"Really? I mean, a real one?"

"Yes. They exist. Anyway, it would take too long to explain now, but the man has been a good friend. He needs help fighting some killer Serpents who serve Satan. Christ gave me a task. If I fulfil it by helping John, the man, I will be rewarded with salvation. I know it! I need you to come with me."

"Ha! A pretty speech. We are simply the creation of the Devil. It's about time you faced it. All other vampires do. You are the only one who thinks he might be good. I wish I had never met you. My life was simple before you. Now, it's too complicated. Do you still not see that we are his servants? There is *no* light for us, *no* salvation! I still want to die. And Madame Guillotine is the best way! I asked you a hundred times to kill me. You wouldn't do it. I'm going. My mind's made up. Now leave me alone!"

"You're young, idealistic. I know that."

"Ha! What are we but a race of parasites? We have *nothing* to be proud of. Name me one thing?"

"But you *do* need something to believe in. I know it."

My words met with no response. For a while, I was at a loss. I had to dredge my very soul for anything that might persuade my friend to live. A faint memory came back to me, of sitting on my father's lap and listening to a story every night. I never believed half of what my father told me. Much less did I respect him. But I needed something now.

"My father used to tell me a story," I began. "In the beginning, Men warred among themselves when tribe met tribe. They were hunter-gatherers. But a few leaders feasted on blood alone. Nutritious and abundantly available to the powerful, it was an attractive diet. After a time, these men attained special powers of movement and stealth. It was apparent that they represented a kind of super-species, that is a species, some would say parasitic, it's true, which could exist alongside the donor-species and attain supremacy."

With time on their hands, they learned many things, and they became great leaders. They learned not only how to rule men but about astrology, navigation, a mode of movement which resembled time-travel and about the secret history of the world. Their lives became extended, and they learned to extend them further, eventually to the length of many generation of normal men. Some travelled widely and founded a great city in modern-day Peru."

They lived peacefully alongside their brethren, because they encouraged the enterprising to join their ranks. They were benevolent leaders, for the most part. They preferred neither night nor day but were more comfortable than other men at night, because their eyes adapted better to low-light conditions. Their ears too changed, becoming more sensitive and slightly pointed, to capture more sound in the darkness. Gradually they began to call themselves El-yr, 'The Long-lived,' and normal men they called El-bass, 'The low Ones'. Their arrogance was to cost them dearly."

Trouble came for the elite, who were now known as Valyr, 'Vain of years,' by men of normal years, when a small group of rebels in what is now China, escaped and started a community in an isolated valley. They were forgotten by the El-yr, and some learned to plant seeds and wait for them to ripen. They began to shun meat and led a settled life. A few ventured to other lands, and the techniques of agriculture were secretly spread."

By now the El-yr had established a great city in

modern Peru and this became their … focal-point. When there was finally an uprising in the East, great armies of the El-yr had no trouble putting them down. They wanted a return to the ways of farming animals for this provided them with the most easily available source of blood. But the tide of change was against them."

From a distant star, called Anu by its planets' inhabitants, came an alien species. They were pirate traders who travelled in space and time but arrived too early on Earth and became stranded."

They became known as the Anuk-una since Anuk was much like their own word for wolf, Atuk. Anuk-una later become corrupted to Anukuna. They were taller, stronger than men and with heads like jackals. but they were also God's creatures. They came seeking iron, and at first, they were willing to trade. But of course, the Valyr, as our kind were now named by all others, wanted control of the trade. When the Anukuna began to deal directly with bases, seeing an opportunity for conquest, the Valyr opposed them and war was begun. For nearly a thousand years war raged all over the inhabited Earth. Wherever they could, the Anukuna sought the aid of bases and finally the Valyr were hounded to their last stronghold, the city in Peru."

Here they were finally beaten and fled to the hills and into the night. There's no time now, but I will tell you the rest of the story later. Anyway, the short version is that the city was eventually destroyed.

Men now called the broken city Yampir, 'Golden City of the El-yr,' in memory of its might, and its rulers became ghosts in the night. The name vampira was whispered whenever they were mentioned."

So you see, once we were a great race, almost gods. My grandfather's name was Chariltheos. 'Theos' means 'God.'"

I looked up. Claude's face seemed brightly lit, as if he were smiling at the sun, something men often do, but vampires do not. But then his face darkened into a scowl.

"Ach! Fairy tales. We were never gods! There is nothing in there to say *we* were the creation of God anyway! But I wouldn't mind meeting a werewolf."

***

In Jerusalem, John found himself at the bottom of a long, rock-cut series of steps. Noticeably cooler than the City above, the cavern he stepped into was lit by oily torches. Orange and yellow light flickered on the rough-cut limestone walls.

"Could be a quarry," John thought.

Looking more closely at the rock floor, he could see lines of wagon ruts from a wide, rising tunnel to the left. Then ended in a massive set of black, wooden doors, seemingly of ebony. Around them, piles of crates, some broken.

"But those doors would open onto the street! I didn't see any entrance. Must be blocked off."

As he looked more closely at the walls, John could see that the wide tunnel walls were stained from many hundreds of years of water drainage, while the narrow stairwell looked recent. Another wide tunnel opposite also ended in wooden doors. Only the tunnel to the right offered a way forward, but it filled John with a black dread. The fear of something unknown, senseless, reasonless, emanated from it. With his heart in his mouth, John stumbled forward.

The tunnel, with passing places wide enough for two carts, sloped ever downward until John was sure he must be under the Temple. It turned back on itself and dove deeper into the Earth. Along the right side of the main tunnel, other smaller shafts with steps led toward the surface, but each was blocked by a wooden door after only ten feet.

"Getting hotter!" John muttered to himself.

He became slowly aware of a woman's hysterical scream within his head. It was joined by other voices which veered up and down the register insanely and seemed to draw his will from John' body. The howling choir made him want to close his eyes. Several times, he did and wondered if it was him that screamed, but when he opened his eyes, the voices would disappear, and the tunnel seemed quiet again. Just for a moment.

He guessed himself to be something like 500 feet below ground level when the tunnel again turned east and opened into a wide space. Either side of the tunnel were row upon row of crates, stacked almost to the ceiling.

John leaped behind a crate when he heard slow footsteps approaching. Peering out he saw a creature like no other; about the height of a twelve-year old, it looked like grotesque offspring of a man and a salamander. Yellow, with black stripes from head to tail, it walked on its legs like a human but leaned forward. Several more came into view and filed past.

When they had passed, John crept on.

'What *were* they?' John wondered. 'How could they exist so late and yet not be known about in the 20th Century?'

Every step he took, his feet felt heavier. Every step seemed to take an eternity. The insane howling in his head grew louder and louder. It threatened to take away his own sanity forever.

Somebody yelled something in a guttural language unfamiliar to John. With nowhere to hide, he prepared to brazen it out.

Into sight came a whole gaggle of the salamander creatures. They walked straight past John without stopping. Only one glanced up at the stranger. Its red eyes were vacant and dumb and showed no interest in John.

A little further on, the tunnel divided into two. The one to the left was narrower and descended more steeply.

By now, John was sweating profusely with the heat, which seemed to blast from both tunnels.

John continued down the larger tunnel. It began to widen out before suddenly forming a bottleneck between two flattened plinths of rock. Atop each, was a warrior dressed in armour complete with a twin-horned helmet. The armour was burnished, like bronze, but bore strange designs and decoration. The figures stood at least eight feet tall and bellowed instructions in strange and guttural tongue to someone, or something, beyond. Over the din in his head, John could hear the clamour of other voices and crates being slammed against each other on the other side of the plinths.

Since they were turned away, John risked creeping up to the plinths to get a better look beyond. The tunnel ran on to a precipice, crossed by a single span of a huge bridge. Before the precipice, groups of the salamander creatures were being whipped by human foreman into stacking crates. On the left side the tunnel stood a double set of wooden doors, big enough to admit one of the black, solid-wheeled carts that sat outside the doors. These were being loaded with the crates.

But John's attention was fixed on the bridge. The chasm below it seemed bottomless. Reaching down from the ceiling, was a flat, inverted platform of a few acres, somewhat like a giant stalactite, of limestone rock inside a cavern the size of a modern football stadium. The nearest half of the bridge itself was supported on pillars that were angled to reach the near side of the chasm. But similar pillars on the far side descended from the roof of the cavern! What was more, John could see figures walking across the first half of the bridge normally but then walking around the parapet to continue on the bottom of the bridge and reach the flat plateau!

As he watched, a wagon rolled across the bridge, dragged by naked, human slaves. When it reached the halfway point, the driver steered the wagon over the edge of

the bridge and round to the underside!
Below the central plateau of the cavern was
a giant, inverted dome. Another
extraordinary aspect of the cavern was that
its surfaces were smooth and intricately
decorated with columns and recesses. It
looked as if an ancient cathedral or mosque
had been encased in rock and suddenly
vanished, leaving its shape impressed on the
rock. Nowhere, could John see any sign of
defect or workman's tools.

"Alice: Through the Looking Glass!" John
told himself.

He backed away and retraced his steps. He
turned into the smaller, steeper tunnel and
took a deep breath.

The air in the tunnel was closer and the
light was completely red.

As John descended further, the feeling of
claustrophobia grew until he found it almost
impossible to put one foot in front of the
other.

When he judged that the tunnel had reach
the edge of the chasm, the tunnel ended in a
small landing. To his left, doubling back,
was a stairwell with stone steps. But the
floor was smooth, and the steps were on the
ceiling.

John approached the steps and felt himself
become lighter. His organs seemed to be
floating inside him. The feeling was not so
different from being in love.

In the wall, on the nearside of the steps
were a few more rock-cut steps. John placed
his feet on these and found that he could
walk up the wall to the steps on the

staircase.

"This is the craziest thing I have ever done. What kind of place is it where gravity is reversed? Am I dreaming?"

The urge to turn back and wait for help was almost overpowering, but John knew time was running out. Georgina should have already been somewhere in Jerusalem and he had to find her. She had only hours to live.

Down the staircase, he stumbled, ignoring his own pain. Working out his orientation, John estimated that he was now moving north.

It wasn't long however, before the tunnel turned to the left. John had to remind himself that 'left' meant 'right' in the bizarre complex of tunnels.
"I must be far, far below the Temple and crossing beneath or at the north end of the chasm."

What John most dreaded, came into view. The tunnel opened out again and was flanked on both sides by stone plinths, topped with similar warriors to those he had seen earlier. Beyond them, thick, white columns stretched up, or down, to a vaulted ceiling, of similar workmanship or design to that of the giant cavern. But this was on a lesser scale. This space was more akin to a hall or theatre.

But John could only see the ceiling. Somehow, he had to get past the guards.

John began to focus on his deep anger. He tried to imagine himself gaining the strength of a wolf. But nothing happened.

As he waited, desperately, John could see no way of getting past them. To attack them was futile. Even if he could kill one, it would be like stirring up an ant's nest. He prepared for the only plan that occurred; to create a diversion. From his purse, he quietly pulled a few shekels and held them in his fist. But John became aware of a commotion building on the other side of the plinths. The furthest guards leaped down to intervene.

"It's now or never!" John told himself, before throwing the coins as far back down the corridor as he could. He didn't hear the sound himself, but the second guard swivelled to look.

John crept around the nearside plinth, under the guard of the nearest warrior and sped toward the front of the tunnel. He passed to the right of human slaves, who stared in disbelief at the passing man in the black kudra. The guard who had intervened was too busy talking to a foreman to see what was happing.

The tunnel ended on a wide terrace. John darted around the corner of the tunnel wall and hid behind one of the great stone columns.

"This is impossible! I'm never *this* lucky!"

John darted forward to peer over the terrace balustrade before returning to his column. He saw that near the end of the terrace wing was an iron ladder which led down to a carpeted forecourt. Beyond this was a white balustrade and then a much wider court. A wide circle of more than one hundred naked girls, none older, John estimated, than twenty, slowly filed past the bottom of a grand staircase on the far side of the court. This staircase led up to a very large dais, upon which some kind of winged beast writhed with a naked woman. Two long staircases, either side of the dais, led up and behind the dais and eventually to the roof of the hall.

John watched the girls slowly circulating. He was too far away to see their faces clearly.

'My luck has held so far!' he reflected before running to the ladder and climbing down. The balustrade beside the central court offered little cover, but John could see that most of the guards, both human and monstrous, and indeed most of the working population of the great hall, were behind the balustrade, preoccupied. On the other side of the main court, between the dais and the two staircases, there was a narrow recess, somewhere he could hide. He leaped over the balustrade and ran across the court to the recess.

He watched the girls as they filed past, not more than twenty feet from him.

All the girls stared at the floor, but one girl glanced up. She was achingly beautiful. Her body was less curvy than John remembered it, but she was tall and elegant. Her raven black hair was long, her gorgeous eyes the colour of cinnamon. Her face suddenly looked familiar.

"Georgina!" John hissed.

***

In Paris, I was relieved to finally win Claude's interest.

"I can't get you out of here. You haven't yet learned how to take other forms," I told Claude. "You should have listened to me. When are they taking you out?"

"My execution is at eight in the morning."

"That doesn't give me much time to plan this. Don't worry, I will rescue you before the blade falls."

"Just one condition if you want me to come on this mad adventure."

"Yes?"

"Time's up!" the guard yelled, punctuating this by spitting out apple pips.

"Just one minute!" I yelled back.

I nodded to Claude.

"I am only staying there for one hour. If I don't meet this friend of yours or get involved in something that is going to change my life, I want to be back here in time to be executed; it was very difficult to get arrested. Agreed?"

"Claude. You are crazy. That puts me in a very difficult position. That will mean arriving there later, but I promised my friend I would be back sooner!"

"Agreed?"

"Very well. Agreed."

As I walked through night time Paris to Claude's room, I hoped that John would still be in my room three hours after I left him. Any later, I dare not arrive for fear of letting him down. Any earlier, and I risked losing the trust of Claude. Being caught between the demands of two friends was not a dilemma I had ever faced before, but the novelty, I found, quickly wares off.

Of course, I could leave Claude in Jerusalem, but I

would need to train him how to move through time, and even if I didn't help him come back, he would probably try on his own and might splatter his soul across the whole of time.

I reached his garret room and threw myself on his lice-ridden bed. The windows were fast shut but still didn't keep out the stench of decaying copses.

Lucky that vampires don't have to worry about hygiene.

I woke up, thinking about endlessly washing. Dawn was breaking outside. I had work to do.

"Damn!"

I could see had made a bad mistake. I had nothing for Claude to wear in Jerusalem. I also needed a pair of pistols, perhaps two pairs.

A clock, with three legs, on Claude's mantelpiece told me it was 7.22 am. Allowing for inaccuracy, it still left me plenty of time.

I waved down a fast carriage toward the Place de la Révolution [2], where the executions all took place.

A few streets short of the square, I alighted, leaving a package of my Jerusalem cloths and blades on the back seat, and paid the driver to turn around and wait for three hours.

It wasn't hard to find two pairs flintlock pistols; I chose short barrelled ones, because I wasn't interested in accuracy, and they were less expensive.

I soon found myself waiting near the front of a large crowd in the Place de la Révolution, witnessing the first beheading by guillotine. I have witnessed many deaths, most inflicted by my hand, but my stomach turned when I saw the look of horror on the victim's faces. None were ready to die.

At last I saw a waggon arrive, carrying Claude. He was seated, hands bound, with five other condemned citizens.

When his turn came, he glanced about him on his way to the platform, and I waved at him. He nodded once.

For concealment, I had placed myself three rows back. I surged forward and leaped onto the platform, at once allowing myself to cast the cloak. Pushing a soldier from the platform, I slashed Claude's bond with a knife and drew two of the pistols from my belt.

"Cast the cloak!" I yelled at Claude

I aimed at one of the remaining soldiers, on the platform near the guillotine, and fired a shot. A neat hole appeared in his breastplate. I aimed the second shot just above the crowd and fired. Pandemonium broke out. In the chaos, I handed the two pistols to Claude and led him through the crowd, toward the waiting carriage.

"Arrêtez! Arrêtez!" the soldiers yelled, but they dare not fire into the crowd. We weaved and ducked, and before we knew it, we were safely at the carriage. I stuck my two pistols into my belt and yelled:

"Drive."

I didn't waste any time. As soon as we alighted from the carriage, I led Claude to the cobbled courtyard where I had arrived.

"When I tell you to, run. Hold my hand and imagine this picture. It's the best I could do. There are other ways, but this is the simplest."

From my pocket, I unfolded a print of a painting I had found, of Jerusalem at the time of Iesous and put it in Claude's hand.

"Memorize it. Ready! Run!"

We ran toward the far wall, the edifice of a building containing many apartments. In the lowest window, a washing woman watched us running toward her, aghast. I thought we weren't going to make it, but just before we hit the bricks, everything went dark.

We landed together on the hill outside Jerusalem, and both fell to the dirt, exhausted.

After a few minutes to get our breaths back I led Claude to a place near the Gate of the Essenes and told him to hide in the bushes. It didn't take me long to buy a very inexpensive kudra, get Claude to put it over his own clothes and lead him to my room.

Imagine my disappointment and fear when I found the room empty.

Some butter on a plate in direct sunlight still had not melted.

"We must have missed John by minutes!"

***

In the subterranean cavern, John didn't wait for Georgina to go round the circle again. He ran forward and pulled her to the recess. The other girls looked up in terror but quickly closed the gap in the circle.

"Georgina! It's me. John!"

"Jean? Is that you? You fool! Get away from here! They will see you and kill you!"

"I haven't come all this way to leave without you. Come on. I know how to get out."

"You are crazy! You can't just walk out of here! Some of us have tried."

"How long have you been here? You look about twenty."

"Yes. It is the effect. I must have been here at least twelve hours although it's hard to tell in here. Time seems to stop. They say that time repeats every three days."

"Long enough for you to die."

"I hardly recognised *you*. We look the same age!"

"But we both only have hours to live. You know we cannot get younger than sixteen and live?"

"I know. I don't want to live. You know that."

"That was a long time ago."

"A few weeks ago, in Ireland."

"Oh, *that*!. We have to run. Come on."

Georgina pulled back on John's hand. "I'm a witch, a succubus. I'm not just your little French Georgina. I have a destiny, and that is to give myself completely to the Master.

"Satan? No, your destiny is something else."

The certainty in John's eye must have caught Georgina's attention. She stopped pulling and drew him down, to sit on the floor.

"Jeez, it's hotter than Hell down here," John said. "And those voices in my head! Do they never *stop*?"

"They will find you very soon," Georgina told John. "They may kill me too for speaking with you. Jean! Jean! Always, you are fighting for my soul. I love you. Why do you always turn up too late?" She shook her head. "There are many things you don't understand. There are some things I know … ." Georgina shook her head. "I have given myself to the Master of All, many times but never completely. Always he sent me back to do his work for him. Always he promised me that one day I would be his, that I am his special one, his favourite. He talked to me, told me his deepest secrets!" For a moment, an agony flickered across Georgina's face. "I know something I might never be able to tell you. But I will tell you some things that might change your mind."

God created twelve Angels to help him. They are: Lucifer, the most high and talented; Jibrail or Michael, the kindness of God; Ruth, who cares for all that grows and must become; Gabriel, the kindness of God; Israfil, God's healing force; Uriel, who leads us to destiny; Samael, the Severity of God; HaMavet, the Angel of Death; Sandalphon, battles Samael and brings mankind together; Jophiel, the beauty and justice of God; Metatron, the Recorder of Deeds and Phenoa, the Eternally Weak."

God knows everything, but he cannot save everyone. When Lucifer went to Hell he took one twelfth of the souls with bodies with him, but these souls kept switching with those in Heaven until God could not distinguish good souls from bad and so didn't know who to exclude from Heaven any more. So he created Earth where he could send all the souls and begin to decide who should be in Heaven and who, in Hell. He created a reflection of Heaven and Hell which was Earth."

There is and has always been only twelve people on Earth. Only the Angels have a real body on Earth, because their spirits are strong enough to be in two places at once, Heaven and Hell. They do not always know what they really are. Some only know once they are woken up. Once they are awake, they can sense when they are in the presence of another. Hence, some know of each other's existence. Some choose to be known, far and wide as powerful men or women; merchants, kings or queens and are known to the others. But some hide away and are not known."

Of those that are known on Earth, some have become lost to memory or obscured. But some are known. In order, they are: unknown, Michael, Atara, unknown, unknown, Theo, unknown, Mara, unknown, Eliam, Hu Hai and Zenobia. They all live on, sometimes taking different names, sometimes choosing rebirth. Lucifer has ever been here, in Jerusalem.

"But I have met a Mara! A strange man, possibly another time traveller! I met him yesterday! Mara bar Serepion."

Georgina smiled at John.

"Oh, this whole idea is preposterous!"

"Not an idea. It's a fact."

"Then you are saying that I am either one of the Angels or that I don't exist! But I think, therefore I *know* I exist!"

"You are a werewolf. You are a spirit created by God. Like vampires, you exist on both planes, because you have a stronger spirit."

"Stronger? Then you are saying that Rose doesn't exist?"

"Perhaps. Of course, she could be one of the twelve and not know it. You wouldn't know. I didn't say other people *don't* exist. I said they are not *real*. They are more like ghosts. You see them on Earth, but they're not really there."

"And my children? And my parents and sisters?"

Georgina looked away and John thought he had caught Georgina out. But then she looked back, and there was yet another knowing smile on her lips.

"You see, death is nothing. Don't fear for me Jean. The world is stranger than you think."

"Is this place Satan's House. Is this Hell?"

"Only the first level. Things are still real here. Bodies can still touch. Up there, things are a lot different." She glanced up at one of the staircases, beside the dais. Now you must … ."

"What?"

Georgina seemed distracted by something behind John. he felt something prod his back and spun round. One of the giant guards was standing over him. Another was prodding John with an oversized spear.

"Had a nice little talk, have we?" the nearest guard said.

His voice had the same, hideously guttural sound I had heard earlier. It was hard to discern his words, and the voice reminded John of the Serpents'. He wondered if it was a Serpent. John glanced at the gap in his helmet, where the face should be, but there was only blank flesh. He, or it, had *no face*!

"It's not good to mess with the Master's property," the empty face continued. I couldn't see how it was making sounds. It glanced at Georgina and grunted: "Get back to the line."

John saw a flicker of fear in Georgina's eye. He reached for her fine wrist, but she slipped past him. He hoped it was to deceive the guards. Around the bottom of the steps, two more guards came into view. John leaped over the low balustrade, only to see a number of other guards lined up against me. He dived for a narrow gap but received a heavy blow on the back from a club of some kind. Feet pinned him to the ground. He was caught!

The guards dragged John, kicking and yelling up the steps and along a long tunnel where increasing heat threatened to roast him.

In that made place, nothing made sense. Whereas, usually on Earth, up meant light and clean air, here, it meant fetidness and dire heat. They threw John into a cell with a mattress and locked the door.

She's scared! Somebody told her to say all that!

John had to strip to his underwear, so that he could think.

Shit! So I really am stuck in a cell, in the first level of Hell. I always knew I would end up here! I have to get Georgina out! But I can't even get myself out now! I don't even have a sword and my powers don't work here. And we both have only a few hours left! Look at me. I look like a teenager. Soon I will start losing muscle mass.

John tried to make light of his situation, but it was becoming direr by the minute.

Without warning, a key turned in the door lock, and the iron door swung open.

"Ruth!" John exclaimed.

The owner of the Third Eye was wearing a tasteful black dress, reminiscent of 20th Century haute couture.

"Did you really think you could wonder around in here without being discovered? My guards were told to let you through. In fact, they did such a good job, I may have to reward them! I never knew they could act!"

"But why?"

"Because I am curious about you. Because I have heard so much about you, watched you for so long, and wondered why there is *so much* interest in you, from all parties."

"It's nice to know I am thought about. But why did you 'bring' me here then? Why couldn't we have talked above your little wine house?"

"Two reasons: first; I wanted to see how you operate, maybe I could use you and second; we can have some fun!"

"Fun?"

"You liked the other night, together, didn't you?"

"A little strange, but I can't deny it was fun … at the time."

"You mean you would rather be playing with your little Georgina now?"

"I would rather be warming my feet by a fire in my house in Nevers right now."

"But you want to save her?"

"It seems you know most of what I am thinking."

"It will never happen! She's too useful to

me. By the way, I know you are wondering; the reason your powers don't work in here is, because we outnumber you hugely. Our powers overpower yours, if I might make a pun."

"'Trump,' you mean?"

"Yes, and my beauty trumps Georgina's. You don't believe me?"

Suddenly, huge black wings sprang from Ruth's back, splitting wide open the back of her dress and leaving her completely naked. John wrote here that she indeed seemed even more beautiful than Georgina. I won't use his exact words!

"Now I see why everything is so hot and red here," John murmured. The words seemed to come out of my mouth of their own volition.

"Yes, you are experienced your deepest feelings. You are far, far inside yourself." She wrapped herself around John and tore away his last bit of cover.

"I see your body liked me, even if you don't! Ruth whispered.

John was caught up in a whirlwind of ecstasy.

"I am going to release your powers, just enough to please *me*," Ruth murmured.

At last, John felt his powers growing, his muscles expanding and fangs extending. He wanted to kill Ruth, but she seemed to control even his muscles. Try as he might, John could not move to do anything other than caress and scratch his lover. Moreover, a feeling like being in love was growing, seeded as it was by the first ache he had felt when he entered Hell's tunnels.

Ruth bit into his neck and then raked his back with her cruel talons. She had become something more akin to a dragon.

The pain in John's back was mixed so completely with pleasure that he yearned for her to cut deeper. He tore a strip of flesh from her leathery flank.

"That's right darling! Tear it away. It's only flesh. Do you like it?"

John wrote later that he had never even dreamed of a pleasure so great, so intense. When they both finally climaxed, it was as if the world, Heaven and Hell no longer existed, only a limitless pleasure.

It seemed like many hours before the waves of pleasure and pain subsided.

John was lying on the mattress, amid a pool of his own blood and Ruth was at the door.

"I would like to meet your Master, if he is available."

"I will give you time to think about things," she murmured. In any case, I haven't decided what to do with you yet. If I don't think of anything in the next few hours, you will be dead, and I am very busy."

***

Chapter Four

Back in Jerusalem, I knew there was only one possible way to find John now. I led Claude to the Third Eye, purchasing a simple sword for him on the way, and entered the courtyard. I searched on the southern wall for a sign in vain.

"I knew it was a stupid idea!" I muttered.

We left the courtyard without buying a drink.

"Where now?" I wondered out loud.

My attention was caught by a scruffy kid, signalling for me to follow him on a street corner.

'Maybe he knows where John is,' I wondered.

"I was paid to give you a message," the little boy whispered into my ear.

As soon as he had told me his message, I ruffled his hair, gave him a shekel and headed back to the viaduct. I soon arrived at the run-down house, where we both peered into the rear courtyard.

"There's the outhouse," Claude declared.

"Yes. No sign of any activity. What do you think?"

"It looks ominous. I'm coming with you."

"But it could be either very dangerous or boring," I told Claude.

"If I don't go with you, I will go home!"

"Alright. Follow me. Cast the cloak!"

We climbed over the low wall and ran to the door. I pulled it, and it swung open. My sixth sense told me there was something very bad at the bottom of the steps that greeted us, but now I had a friend, I didn't want to lose him. I led Claude cautiously down the steps and into a wide cavern.

"What's that?" Claude asked, eyeing a pile of rubble against a wooden structure to our left. I saw another one in a tunnel straight ahead.

"Another entrance. Blocked." I replied. "They could

be useful. There's another. Come on. Obviously, John must have taken this tunnel."

"I don't like it. I know I wanted some action, but it feels bad, very bad."

"I know. It's a good job I can take other forms. I'm not sure you should come Claude."

"I'm fine. For now. It's less risky than the guillotine."

I almost laughed. It was the first joke Claude had cracked for years. It didn't take long to reach the two guards, on their pedestals, mentioned in John's journal. I indicated that we should back off and followed Claude as we retraced our steps to a safe distance.

"I have never seen anything like them!" I whispered. "If I can, I will go on alone in another form. This is as far as you can come. I told you to learn how to change form!"

"Alright! Alright! What do you want me to do?"

"Those blocked exits. Find a way through. And make a barricade across the main tunnel. I don't know if it will help, but if I can get John this far, we'll need all the help we can get. Keep a way open for us to get out. Oh, and if I'm not back in half an hour, get out of here!"

"Right!"

I stripped, handing my clothes, sword and dagger to Claude and set off along the tunnel. With every step I focused harder on having paws, and soon I saw my legs and arms change into those of a large, black dog. I found the fork in the tunnels and picked up a trace of John's scent in the left branch. After a few turns in the tunnel, I came to the landing with the upside-down stairs. With hardly a hesitation, I took them. An animal does what it is able and doesn't think about gravity. I sped past the two guards. Still following John's scent, I leaped over a parapet and then down to a large open space, which I crossed at full pelt. I could hear shouting behind me. A spear missed me by inches and clattered against steps near a giant, winged creature that filled me with dread.

I dared not do more than glance at its ugly shape, but its eyes, burning like fire, bore into mine like steel into butter. I yelped but ran on, up the stairs. Up and up I went.

Something exploded in front of me and the stairwell filled with fire. Without thinking I changed into the form of an owl and just made it through a closing gap in the flames.

I flew on until I reached a line of cells. Suddenly, as if wafted away on an infernal breeze, I could not detect John's scent. I had to check every cell. I knew what I sought was in one of them. I saw John, flew through the grate and alighted on a mattress beside him.

I tried to change back to my human form slowly, so as not to frighten John, but he was in too bad a shape to care much. Deep lacerations extended all down his torso, arms and legs and he had lost a lot of blood. The mattress was soaked.

"Nice trick!" he gasped.

"I learned it from you! What in *Hell* happened to you?"

"Sex!"

"Really? How? Never mind, explain later. I need to get you out of here, but how? Hm"

"I think I can walk." John managed, painfully, to stand up.

"You could have waited for me? I missed you by a few minutes."

"How did you find me?"

"The boy. Can you bend the bars or break the lock?"

"Are you joking? Anyway, my powers don't work in here. This is Hell. Or the first level. Have you figured that out yet?"

"No. But I can believe it. Being a vampire, I am probably pretty immune from anything the Devil cares to think up. But this place makes me shake. Georgina?"

"They have her. She is terrified. I have spoken to her."

Speech seemed to come with difficult to John, so I let him be.

"Wait here." I told him.

"They're coming!"

"I know."

We could both here the stamping of many metal-booted feet approaching. With a great effort, I changed to a bear and rammed the door with my shoulder. It shook but held. I backed off and rammed it again. The lock buckled, leaving a gap between the door and its frame, but it took one more barge to break the lock entirely and open the door.

Bellowing with mock rage, I charged the two guards, who were struggling to draw their swords in the cramped passage. I smashed one aside before he could take a swipe at me, but the other drew a long line of blood from my back with his blade. It stung, but I could still move. I turned and stood up on my hind legs. Still, he was as tall as me. But not so heavy. He was singularly determined and didn't hesitate to swing his sword at my jaw, but I piled all my weight on top of him. He went down. While I tried to find a weak point in his armour, John drove his sword through the vacant flesh where the guard's face should have been.

More feet could be heard coming.

"The other way?" John yelled.

"Blocked," I growled. He probably didn't understand me, so I shook my head.

"On my back, I indicated with my paw. I immediately changed to a huge bull and waited for my rider. As four other guards turned the corner, into our section of the passage, I drove at them. They stood no chance. I drove on and on, through perhaps a dozen of the attackers, until we emerged at the end of the corridor. I relaxed and changed back to my own form, dumping John on the floor.

"That's it. I am too weary for more," I panted.

"We came that way!" John yelled, pointing.

"I hear them. More are coming from there."

I had small cuts all over my face and shoulders, and my back was oozing blood, but I was still able to run.

"This way!" I shouted, pointing the other way. We ran until we came to the stop of a mirror-image staircase of the one I had flown up. We both looked at each other and shouted together:

"Down!"

"Georgina!" John cried. "We must find her!"

"No. Later. We have to get out. If we can. I have a friend waiting to help." John nodded, "Just a bit further!" I lied.

I remembering yelling to John something like, "So far, so good!" but moments later we reached the bottom of the steps and emerged to the right of the dais. A single, winged Serpent, towering above me, with eyes like fire and red scales of the screaming damned, stood guard over the dais. Upon a giant, silken bed, slept a gorgeous, naked brunette. I feared the worst.

"Georgina!" John yelled for the second time. Her name was beginning to irritate me.

"Leave her John.

The Serpent and John sized each other up.

"Chalcathgna?" John barely whispered.

The response of the beast was awful to hear, the words barely audible behind a guttural hiss of thousands of souls crying for death:

"The same. You want her?"

"Nice trick; putting here here!" I whispered to break

the spell the beast was casting over John. His eyes had glazed over.

"Was it you at Bouvines?" he asked the Serpent.

"No. Another. You killed him. Now there are only nine of us." The beast seemed strangely weary.

"But he showed himself as a man when he fought me. Fight me on equal terms.

"That's not my choice to make. This time I am to stop you leaving."

Each time the beast spoke, my flesh crawled, and my legs felt weak. John seemed more steadfast.

"And what if I just go?" John asked.

"But can you do it?" the Serpent countered.

I gripped John's wrist and felt him shudder with an effort.

"We're going!" he hissed.

But as we turned away, the Serpent let out an enraged howl, and its head darted toward John. With all my speed, I lunged for John. With my heightened awareness, from the corner of my eye I noticed Georgina was on her knees and muttering some kind of prayer or incantation. But that damned snake was too fast for me. Within the blink of an eye, it closed its great jaw around John's head while embracing him with his wings.

'This is it! He's had it now!' I thought.

But John seemed to have anticipated the move. Into the snake's mouth went not only John's head but his sword. I heard John moaning as the jaws squeezed his skull, but then there was a sickening roar from the beast, and John's blade emerged from its snout.

The Serpent released its grip and snapped back its head.

John fell to the floor. His head was bloody, some of his hair torn away, and strips of flesh hung from his scalp.

The beast shook its head once. I had just enough time to grab the sword from the floor before the Serpent lunged again. This time it swung its head around to grip John's chest laterally. It released its grip and moved slightly before gripping again. I could see what it was doing, trying to puncture his heart with its great fangs.

I brought the sword's blade down on the Serpent's upper body. The blade drove deep into the Serpents sickening, red flesh, but the body's diameter was at least four feet, so I made little impression. Even the flesh inside its body was red. Human bodies seemed to writhe within, some of them cut by my blow. I could still see Georgina murmuring her incantation but with no apparent effort.

'Unless she's controlling the beast,' I wondered.

But the Serpent was sinking its fangs into John's chest. I had to act. I dived toward my friend and hacked at the snake's mouth with the blade. By pure luck, the blade caught the left fang of the beast. I felt it engage and bite into the hard material. I sawed at the tooth and twisted the gilt handle. I heard something snap and, again, the Serpent pulled away from John's body. As it slid its lower jaw out from under his body, John rolled over, and for the first time, I could see that he was still alive. He stared straight at me.

The Serpent now only had one long fang left. Its dripping saliva was the colour of blood.

"You're fast valyr," It took a moment before I knew the beast was talking to me. "Keep back, or I'll have your soul too."

"I thought I already *was* damned!" I replied.

"Chalcathgna!" the girl suddenly murmured. Only my keen ears and those of the Beast would have heard her, but the Serpent hesitated. It was a chance.

I crawled forward, grabbed John's wrist and started to drag him away from the dais.

"Chalcathgna!" Georgina moaned. "I command you to stop!" She reached out and touched the Serpent's tail.

For just an instant, its eyes became yellow, and it screamed with a pain that must have touched the very spires in Heaven.

I threw myself on the ground in fear of what would happen. I heard a distant rumble. Something was falling. Or coming. I couldn't decide which was better.

Even with my eyes closed, I began dragging John again.

Georgina screamed, "No!"

I had to look, and I saw the Serpent lunge once more with its remaining fang. I yanked John away as hard as I could, and I almost made it! But the Serpent drove its fang straight through my friend's foot. In an instant, the fang drew away, and the Serpent backed off. It hissed:

"I have you now John! You will soon be one of us!"

The Serpent seemed to be struggling against something. It curled its wings up and lay beside the girl as if going to sleep. She was still chanting some unearthly incantation, occasionally punctuated with the snake's name.

"Come on John!" I yelled.

I dragged him across the court and up to one of the ladders. If I could have changed then, I would gladly have done so.

Already, a host of perhaps a thousand guards and strange yellow and black striped creatures was pouring into the court from different entrances and down the stairs. Above me, the balcony was filling with beasts. From the corner of my eye, I saw other winged Serpents flying into the court.

There seemed absolutely no hope of escape.

I doggedly clasped John's arms around my neck and climbed with one hand. By the time I reached the top, some of those ten-foot guards were already eyeing me for their victim.

But then, from the tunnel ahead came the screams of monsters in pain. Doubt spread on the faces of those above me.

They turned away from us, toward the greater danger.

I reached the columned balcony and lay there, gasping. I could go no further.

"If this is death," I thought, "it's been worth it."

The screaming of guards grew greater, and then a fireball burst from the tunnel. Inside the fireball, I could make out the shape of a wagon, drawn by those striped creatures, and, on the wagon, sat Claude. Now, vampires are fairly resistant to fire, but make no mistake, Claude was burning. But he was laughing.

"Come on!" he yelled to me, whipping the creatures to turn the wagon around.

They seemed senseless to their own pain or whoever commanded them.

I staggered to my feet and dragged John between the stream of guards that were throwing themselves over the balcony edge to escape the fire. The salamander ignored me and burned like torches.

"But he'll burn!" I yelled.

"I thought of that. On the back. Barrel of water. I thought it would be useful.

"He'll drown!"

"He won't have time!"

With my last burst of energy, I hauled john through the tailgate and into the barrel of water which was lashed to the wagon. I fell over as we lurched off, hauled by those sleepy salamanders. We surged down the tunnel in a ball of fire, slashing and kicking at our attackers when they dared to penetrate the flames. The salamanders were agile enough to step over any obstacle and dragged the wagon, bouncing, over dead and dying bodies.

I was beginning to feel uncomfortable when we reached the bottom of the staircase, which turned the tunnel upside down. Our path had been strewn with dead and burning bodies. But even now, some fought, even as they died.

As Claude hauled the barrel containing John to safety and doused himself with water, I had to parry the blows of two giant guards and drive my blade through the chest of another.

"Come on!" Claude yelled, carrying John down the steps. "We have friends waiting."

Never did I hear sweeter words. I doused myself in water and ran up the steps. At the top, I continued, onto the ceiling, which of course became the floor. I caught up the Claude, and together, we dragged John toward the tunnel entrance.

However, our ordeal wasn't over. When we reached the joining of the two tunnels, from our left came Satan's hordes.

They were close on our heels and gaining as we struggled toward the place where I had left Claude.

"Barricade!" was all Claude had the breath to shout.

I guessed what he meant. I doubled my effort, and as we came around a turn, I saw a row of crates across the floor. One crate was pulled back, leaving us a way through. I recognised the white-haired knight behind a crate, but he was not alone. Either side of him were three other tall men.

"We … won't make it!" I shouted.

"We will! Don't be … so … morb-!" Claude gasped.

His words were cut short by a spear which pierced his charred arm, which was holding up John. The force of the blow spun him round.

"Run!" I told him. We were only a short stone's throw from the barricade, and it looked like we might make it. Claude ran on and the knight threw him another sword.

Something hit me in the back, and I dropped like a stone. Great gloved hands grabbed at John and me from behind, but I didn't let go.

"Get off us you filth!" I growled.

They began screaming. At first, I thought they were scared of me but then I simultaneously saw a spear penetrating the neck of one and felt the whizzing of spears passing over my head.

I kicked at the faceless head of one guard and slashed the arm of another from its shoulder and then staggered to my feet. I dragged John's limp and bloody body to the barricade.

"Come on!" the men ahead yelled.

With one last, desperate burst of effort, I was through the gap, and the barricade was closed.

The first wave of monsters hit the crates like a tidal-wave, pushing some aside, clambering on others, but the knights fought bravely, and some were able to change to werewolves this far away from the halls of Hell.

"Get out!" John's grandfather, the knight in a crusader tunic, shouted. We'll follow you! The gates are blocked beyond."

For the first time, I noticed that one of the great gates had been opened, but only limestone blocks and rubble could be seen beyond.

John began to stir. He shook his bloody head, so I pulled him to his feet.

"Can you walk?" I yelled. "Come on!"

Half supporting, half dragging John, I climbed the short flight of steps to the door in the outhouse. In another few moments, we were outside. It was even darker than the torch-lit tunnel.

We made our way to the end of the street to wait for

the others.

They arrived in dribs and drabs, all of them weary and many wounded. John's grandfather was the last one out. He looked half the age he was when I first saw him. His hair was even brown, but he looked incredibly weary.

"Grandad Hugo!" John murmured. "How many?"

John was lying against a wall. Hugo took his grandson in his arms.

"We lost three!" Hugo replied. "Four left, not including you! John! John! What have they done to you?"

"I … I am very tired. I don't know why. It was Chalcathgna. I think he did something to me."

"I can see that!" Hugo replied. "Let's get you out of here. We have rooms nearby. They won't come outside, not yet. Their Master needs to give them permission for that. And they need a plan, I think."

"Here is your sword. Thank you for letting me borrow it," I said. I expected each of John's breaths to be his last. His wound looked fatal; deep lacerations to his face and scalp, down his back and chest and deep puncture wounds on both sides of his torso. It was a miracle none had punctured his lungs. I assumed they hadn't, because his breath was coming more easily now.

"No, I mean … "John began as two knights lifted him and carried him toward our refuge.

"Sh! Not now!" Hugo ordered.

People drew back and put their hands over their mouths when the saw us, partly through shock at John's state and partly from fear of such strangely attired and terrifying armed men.

***

Two of Hugo's knights had considerable skill as physicians and worked on John while he was propped up on a mattress. While they stitched, dabbed and bandaged, I kept him supplied with the strongest wine available to kill the pain.

After nearly an hour, he was beginning to look more human and began to talk:

"We have to have a plan?"

"What for?" I asked

"Going back in."

"You are joking?"

"No. I have to save Georgina."

"I must admit, she's quite a woman."

"She saved me."

"Well," I replied, smiling. "She helped a lot!"

"Yes. Thanks Zosimyache. But you *didn't* save my life."

I must have looked angry. John drew me down to whisper in my ear:

"I tried to tell Hugo on the street. That Serpent injected me with something. A poison. I can feel it working its way round my body."

"It tried to pierce your heart but missed. It may have done so in your foot. I can't be sure. It's a wonder you're alive at all. Why don't you wait? If you survive tonight, you may live!"

"No. There's no time. And I'm sure. I am dying. Didn't I tell you? One of us must die. To pay the debt for Georgina."

I ignored John.

Several of the knights were getting nervous.

"What is he saying?" Hugo asked me.

"He wants to go back in, to get that succubus, Georgina."

To my surprise, Hugo nodded slowly and murmured:

"Yes. That may be his destiny. I fear, from the blackened flesh around the wound on his foot, that he has Chalcathgna's poison in his veins."

"And that means?"

"Who knows? But it's not good."

"Chalcathgna said – if you can call that gurgle speech – that John would become one of them."

"Oh."

"It's probably true granddad," John said. "Some of the Serpents were recruited from werewolves. They have always wanted me. Or He has always wanted me. You must let me do one last thing before I go. I *must* save Georgina."

"Who am I to argue," Hugo replied. "You are the supreme werewolf. There will never be another like you. Perhaps, if you complete this task, they will not have your soul. I just wish I knew why she is so damned important."

"Me too," I echoed.

"I don't know," replied John.

***

Hugo seemed to be the leader of the other Ordo Lupus members. He was certainly the tallest and had that giant, silver sword that John had told me about, thought I hadn't seen him wield it yet. He issued instructions to the other men to spread out and find provisions and equipment for the attack. Then he turned to John:

"Why don't we wait here John? They will come out, seeking us, soon enough. There is still time. If they are not here by an hour before noon, *then* we can go in."

His entreaty fell on deaf ears.

"What time is it?" John asked.

"Roughly six o'clock. It will be dawn soon."

"Listen. Georgina told me something. I want to know what you both think. Georgina told me that there are only twelve *real* people on Earth, that most of us live in either Hell or Heaven and are represented here by a sort of ghost. They are the twelve Angels but not always aware of what they are at first. She excluded werewolves and vampires, saying that they have stronger spirits, and like the twelve Angels, can be in either Heaven or Hell at the same time as on Earth.

Why she thought it so important to tell me this when our lives were both in dire peril, I don't know. But I questioned her, asking if therefore my wife might not exist! Georgina was at pains to point out that Rose did exist but not necessarily physically on Earth. She defeated my reasoning at every turn. I have to admit, it has a ring of truth about it, for me. What do you both think?"

"You should be resting, not thinking about philosophy!" I countered.

"No time for resting now. We have one hour before we go back in. *What* do you both think?"

John was insistent, but I hadn't yet formed an opinion. Hugo replied first:

"There have been rumours of this since as long as man has existed. It's only whispered in the shadows though. The Church abhors such talk and punishes those that believe it. The CPV, as you called them in our book, are particularly severe with anybody that preaches the idea."

"But what do *you* think?" John countered.

"Well, it has some merit, as an idea, but I am a fledgling werewolf, so I cannot feel these things. You know, you look like one of those mummy things in a horror film!"

"Thanks. My head is killing me. And you, Zosimyache? What do you think?"

"I suppose they take up positions of great power and influence, kings, queens and the like?"

"Some, apparently. The others hide. Lucifer hasn't revealed himself. Some find each other, and then their names are known. Mara was one. I think we met him at Golgotha; Mara bar Serapion."

"A time traveller? Yes, that makes sense. Ha! So I have met an Angel! Ha, did you hear that Claude? But, as Hugo says, it is a remote idea for me. It doesn't concern my own kind. I don't see how it concerns *you*."

"Only in that it offers a glimpse behind the curtain of death. I am going there soon. I would like to think I will meet all these extraordinary people."

There was no answer to that. I left John to get some rest. When I returned, a few minutes before we were due to leave, John was asleep.

"He was sweating and weary," Hugo explained. "He is suffering from extreme hydration, probably mixed with shock. He fell asleep. I don't want to wake him yet."

"Let him. Do we have all we need yet?"

"No. There are few shops and workshops open yet. For some reason, our allies seem to have grown thin on the ground. We need food, daggers, spears and swords, on and torches."

"Will you get all that in time?"

"I don't know, but if not, there are our secret weapons." Hugo pointed to the mattress, and one of his men lifted its edge. He held up three M16 rifles and a Colt .45 pistol. "And these," he added, pointing to two barrels, labelled 'gunpowder,' in the corner of the room

"Good!" I replied. "But couldn't you bring more guns?"

"We had to move fast. Otherwise we wouldn't have been here in time. We were lucky to get the gunpowder!"

Over the next thirty minutes, Hugo's men all returned.

There were enough daggers, swords and spears for our needs. There were even a few slings though only one man knew how to use one. He gave a quick training session in the courtyard. Everyone spoke in hushed tones. The feeling of tension was palpable.

John was beginning to wake up. The first thing he asked was:

"What time?"

Not much before nine," Hugo replied, holding up his hand to John's imminent protest. "You needed sleep. Can you walk?"

John struggled to his feet and smiled.

"I can, but my feet are cold. Are we almost ready?"

Everyone except John continued to whisper, even though he was now awake.

"We have guns" I told him. "But we are outnumbered.

"Why didn't you use them in the tunnel?" John demanded of Hugo.

"We did, once. We fired one shot after you left. I don't think you can scare those guys in armour but it made them hesitate long enough for us to get out."

"So there are five of us," John said.

"And twelve Serpents," Hugo added.

"Nine. Chalcathgna told me three are destroyed. Of course, it will be ten if they get me. There's something else. Georgina was trying to tell me something. I don't know what, but I know her well enough to know that she *knows* something. Something very important!"

All the men were now huddled around John. They hung on his every word. I was suddenly aware of Claude pulling my kudra hem. I had forgotten him.

"John," I whispered. "Meet Claude. Without him, neither of us would have escaped."

"Why are you all whispering? I'm not dead yet! Anyway, pleased to meet you Claude!" John held out his hand, and Claude reached forward to take it.

"I am honoure-ed to meet such an estimmed

werewolf!" Claude replied in halting English, clearly dumbstruck by the whole experience. He hesitated before asking, "So what iz ze plan Monsieur?"

"Ah! The plan. Well, we have to fight our way in through the outhouse or those black gates, if we can find them. They will be guarded, but as Hugo says, they are probably getting ready to come out after us now. Maybe we can wait for them to open the gates … . I don't like to ask any of you to accompany me, it's probably suicide, but I'm going in!"

"No John," Hugo replied. "As you probably know, it has been our destiny to arrive here with you. We are all coming with you. We are all prepared to die."

The nods of agreement from John's audience were interrupted by a breathless face at the door. The knight on guard drew his sword and challenged the newcomer who replied in Old French:

"I am Guillaume! The tall man at the door wore a Templar's knee-length white tunic, decorated with a red cross. Underneath the tunic, he wore chainmail leaving only his face visible, which was smeared with sweat and dirt and fringed with a pale beard and a few locks of pale blonde hair. He was grinning. "Truly, I am glad to have found you!"

***

"But I wasn't expecting anybody else!" Hugo protested. I could see he was about to ask his men to restrain the grinning knight in the doorway.

"Wait!" John said. "Why are you here, and how did you find us?"

"Yes, a good question; my name does seem to have been left out of most historical records! I am a member of Ordo Lupus, one of the first members de facto! But I also managed to inveigle my way into the Poor Fellow-Soldiers of Christ and of the Temple of Solomon[3], otherwise know, I believe, as the Knights Templar! De facto, I was one of the original nine members. True, I was a bit young … ." Guillaume seemed a bit embarrassed at his own achievements so simply grinned again.

Hugo and John looked at each other and raised their eyebrows.

"But what are you doing here?" John repeated.

"Ah, yes. I was coming to that … ."

"We don't have much time," John interjected.

"Yes. I can see that. Let's see. We, the first nine, came here in the Year of Our Lord 1119 and were granted access to the caves and tunnels under the Temple Mount. Into the possession of Hugues de Payens, our leader, had come a scroll from an obscure branch of the gnostics called the Ophites[4]. Not much to say about them really except that they venerated the Serpent from the Garden of Eden as a symbol of wisdom."

The text describes a story told by an Ophite called Rubius that his grandfather was one of six Roman soldiers charged with removing the body of Our Lord from his tomb and hiding it in the tunnels under the Mount. Pursuants of Wisdom, Hugues recruited the rest of us to prove whether this was true or not. Of course, we have help in the shape of a description of a wall-marking which marks the body's resting place.

It was I who, quite by accident, found the body in a long off-shoot tunnel from Solomon's Quarry. The only problem was that water was leaking into the makeshift tomb from a cleft in the rock, and the body was too decomposed to ever make much of; there was hardly a bone left. That's why I'm here. Hugues found a reference to the only Temple Gate which led to 1st Century Jerusalem and sent me here to either retrieve the body or at least a verifiable relic."

"And you have this ancient text?" John asked.

"Certainly!"

"We could have helped you identify Iesous. John and I both met him!" Zosimyache interjected.

"If it were true … ." John murmured.

"It's an incredible story!" Hugo protested. "I don't even have proof that you are of Ordo Lupus! Where is the primary Temple Gate?"

"Beauvais Cathedral, although it hasn't been built yet in my time. I have been there … ."

"And what is your family name?" John asked.

"The name I was Christened with was Guillaume de Raysar."

"Good enough for me!" John replied. "You are my ancestor. I have a list somewhere with your name on it but no time now. I am curious; you said water was leaking into the cave?"

"Well, a trickle really. It flows past the cavity in which the body is lain, and down a tunnel to a dead end, where rocks block the tunnel. It's said this was hastily filled in when the Romans burst through to some unspeakable horror."

"Very interesting. I don't know much about Jerusalem, but wasn't there a spring under the Temple? Could the water be from this?"

"You think this could be another way in?" Hugo asked John.

"You mean Hezikiah's Tunnel?" Guillaume replied. "That leads from a spring on the nearby hill outside the City. But it's too far away; about two hundred yards south of the Temple walls."

"There is rumoured to be an ancient spring directly beneath the Temple," said one of Hugo's men. "It dried up in one day, reputedly, during the reign of Hezekiah."

"Hm. What if … it were Satan who redirected it." John suggested. What if it leaks out into the quarry tunnel? What if *there is* another way in? If so, we might even be able to flood the caves with water!" We *have* to try it but it will mean blasting our way through. But is there time?"

"Things *are* rather desperate … ." Hugo added.

"You still haven' explained how you found us," I said.

"I was astonished, yesterday to hear somebody tell me that there was another wearing the Templar Cross. I sought him out and ended up at the Street of the Salt Sellers. This boy came up to me and gave me directions to a house. I asked him why, and he told me that a man with a blue eye and brown eye had told him to pass the message on to a tall man with a white beard and a tunic with a red cross."

"Did you give him any money?" Hugo asked.

"Three shekels."

"I gave him only one! Ha! He must have mistaken you for me! Or chosen to! Clever boy."

"He followed me and together, we watched the house. It wasn't long after that I saw you all emerge, so I followed you here. I wasn't so confident about meeting you though. Perhaps I should have waited."

"Can you show us the way to this quarry tomb?" John asked.

"You look like you *need* some help, young sir! I am not even sure why your men are following such a young man Hugo."

"You don't know who this man is," Hugo retorted. "Of course, he's your *ancestor*, and in a sense, the youngest here, but we all get younger very fast after coming through that Gate. I arrived, this time, aged sixty, and now I look more like forty! John has just been here the longest. John has only hours to live here. Most of us have less than a day to live here, including *you, young sir*!"

"Ah! I thought I noticed something like that! Nevertheless, you look in no fit state for this … mission sir," Guillaume said to John. "I would suggest to your friends that we leave you here and come back later."

"That won't happen," John replied, struggling to his feet. "Are we ready?"

***

To the affirmative, but tense nods, Guillaume led us back to the street. The barrels of gunpowder were wrapped in cloaks, each the sole burden of one man.

John walked beside Hugo while we walked in a long, loose line toward the northern end of the city. Guillaume was practically stepping on John's weary heels. I have never wanted so much to be back home. For a moment, I thought I could smell again the peppery spring heather on the mountainside.

This will be the end of me!

"One thing I don't understand," John murmured to Hugo. "Why is all this focussed on Jerusalem and why now? I mean; why is Satan based here, and why is he so fascinated with Jesus? At least that is what it seems to me."

"I have a theory about that!" Guillaume whispered. He went on without being prompted. "The Devil has probably always been here. Do you know that the 'Jeru' part of the name Jerusalem means 'Dual' or 'built on two hills' and 'Shalem' was the 'God of dusk' in the Canaanite religion. 'Shalem' could also mean the 'Dwelling of peace,' but I think the implication is obvious; that here was a place ruled by a god who was neither completely good nor bad but a 'dualist god.' I even propose that this may have been the origin of 'dualism' and that Satan or the Devil is the ruler of all dualists.

"Then you are saying that the Devil was here first

and perhaps that is why Jesus was born here? Why not the other way round? That the Devil has been waiting for Jesus?"

"That could be!" Guillaume replied. He seemed unable to think what to say next.

We reached the street above the Street of the Salt Sellers and turned into it. Some way along it, Guillaume pointed to a small outcrop of rocks to the left.

"That courtyard. The entrance should be in there."

Two Roman guards stood guard outside a heavy iron grill in a courtyard.

"Now what?" Hugo asked.

"I can deal with this easily," I whispered. "Give me a few moments."

Directly above the iron grill was a rock-face, perhaps thirty feet high, but slightly to the nearside was a ledge only ten feet above the two guards. What was more, I could see an easy way to reach the ledge. Within minutes, I was in place and then leaped down on the nearest guard in dog form. I tore his throat out before he could react. The other guard had a one hand full of figs and the other raised to his mouth, He was too shocked to do anything but drop the figs and reach for his sword. I was upon him well before it left its sheath.

"No! No! No!" was his eloquent protest when my canines penetrated his neck. I transformed back to my usual self, my fangs still immersed in his warm blood. I tasted a sample before dropping him to the ground.

"Later!" I whispered. "It's been a long time since I tasted the blood of Rome."

I waved to the others and John's keen eyes saw that the way was clear. Unfortunately, the guards kept no keys, but a big heave with the hilt of a sword hilt broke the chain around the grill.

We're in!

Every second man drew a torch, made from oil-soaked cloth wrapped around a short staff. They lit them to light our way. From a pouch, Guillaume drew out a tattered piece of parchment and checked his bearings in the flickering torchlight. Ahead of us the tunnel opened up. You could see where large, rectangular blocks of white limestone had been hewn from the cave's walls, ceiling and floor, leaving an uneven surface like an old pavement.

"This way!" he announced, afterwards muttering, "If nothing has changed!"

He led us south, into a vast chamber perhaps 350 feet wide, and on into a series of low tunnels.

"What are we looking for," John asked Guillaume. "Can I see the diagram?"

We huddled round as the knight held up the parchment.

I saw three diagrams and some text. From left to right, I saw: a snake wrapped around a staff underneath what looked like a twelve-pointed star around an eye; a crude depiction of six soldiers carrying a body wrapped in a sheet, with a crucifixion cross as background and a diagram showing a tunnel complex. Centrally placed, underneath the three diagrams was the single Hebrew word, 'ישוע.'

Guillaume pointed to the name and said:

"See, the name, Yeshua. Jesus. These two diagrams on the left are the inscriptions we are looking for," said Guillaume "but they are probably not here yet, given that the crucifixion took place today. Right now, the map is the most crucial. You see there is a long tunnel, with a short tunnel to the right and then the long tunnel branches. To the left, and up an incline, is the tomb. Ahead it eventually ends in the blockage. My memory is a bit vague, but there should be a low tunnel entrance … about here."

Guillaume was triumphantly pointing to an opening, not more than three feet high, which looked to all the world like a dead end, because it was on the extreme left end of a section of tunnel heading west, and one could only see the opposite wall through it.

It was only when Guillaume scrambled through it, sword clanging on the white stone, and disappeared completely that we guessed there was another tunnel to the left, out of sight. We all followed him through. After fifteen feet or so, I was able to stand up again.

"This way," the knight said confidently.

We had passed a few discarded tools, trowels, pick axes and straight irons, which I assumed were used for splitting rock and levering away blocks.

"Pick up a few of those and an axe," Guillaume had told us. "You will need them."

I picked up a straight iron and continued on.

We were moving always south, and I would estimate that we had reached 650 feet or more from the entrance when there was an intersection of four tunnels. Guillaume turned left, into a tunnel which turned back on itself and upward, becoming a flight of stone-cut steps. Again, we reached a junction, and Guillaume turned left, so that we were again moving south, in my estimation.

"We are nearly there!" Guillaume announced.

He stopped at a small, natural grotto which had a large stalagmite in the centre.

"There, now this is the start of the map. We are here!" Guillaume declared, pointing at the bottom end of the long tunnel on the map,

We followed him along the narrowing tunnel until we reached a short tunnel to the right. This led up at a steep angle and was lined with alcoves, as if ready to receive some caskets of the future dead.

"Our tunnel should divide … just here!" the knight

murmured. "Ah! There it is!"

He led us into the left of the two branches, in truth a tunnel that led upwards, almost perpendicular to the previous tunnel. Guillaume stopped about ten feet from the end and sank to his knees. I thought he was tired, but he began wiping away dust from the walls. We all copied him.

"There's nothing here! Guillaume declared after a few minutes.

"No, but this section is wet concrete!" John replied. "Look."

On the south side of the tunnel, about three feet up from the floor, we could all see the impression left by John's hand.

"No name though," John added.

"It looks very similar to when I saw it. But it shouldn't be there!" the knight retorted. When I found it, it was only five feet from the end of the tunnel!"

I rammed my straight iron through the setting concrete, smashing a hole through to an open space. I held a torch to the opening.

"There's a body in there," I reported,

Within a few minutes we had the embalmed body exposed.

Guillaume looked at the linen wrapping around the face nervously.

"Come on man! We don't have much time!" John urged.

Guillaume's lightly touched the linen. His hands were trembling. Drawing his dagger, he cut away some of the linen to reveal a badly scarred face, set sadly in death.

"Is it him?" the knight asked John and I.

"It … looks like him. The wounds are *bad*. Open his eye."

Some of the others looked away. I myself felt

horrified by what we were doing. Guillaume nervously lifted the eye lid.

"Brown eyes, as I remember them," I whispered.

"No blue!" John interjected. "They were definitely *blue*!"

"No John. Brown. And a long face."

"No, a round face!" John said, exasperated.

"Come on now. Can neither of you remember clearly?" Hugo interjected.

"It was dark!" I explained.

"And there seemed to be a bright light around him!" John added. That was the final straw.

"I can't be sure. Neither of us can," I concluded.

"Take a hair sample and skin sample. Your only chance, if you get out of here, is to compare his DNA with a family member," John suggested.

"Come on! Come on!" Hugo said. "This is foolish. It's not Jesus! It never could have been. We have to get on. There's no time!"

He strode back into the long passage and turned left. A few moments later, his voice boomed:

"Guillaume! Let's see that map!"

We followed the young knight into the long passage and saw Hugo with his foot on rubble.

"This passage looks much shorter than on your map," Hugo told Guillaume.

"Yes. It looks like somebody must have taken some rubble away at some time."

"So it is probably something like fifty feet deep, at least?"

"I would guess that is so."

"Right. Then this way is out."

We all went back to the short tunnel and examined the end, which on close inspection proved to be solid rock.

"This was blocked with stone and cement when I

saw it last," Guillaume declared.

"And water was coming through," John asked.

"Yes. Not much. Just a trickle. It flowed down to the blocked tunnel and into the rubble.

"Then this could be the way in," John suggested.

"But 'oo cut through?" Claude asked.

"Must have been us!" John replied. "We have to blast through. It's our only chance."

"But you can't!" Guillaume yelled. "The crypt!"

"We can move the body," I explained.

"But that might cause a Temporal Paradox!" John protested.

"I explained to you; as per eschatology, all is set. Fate is set. There is no Temporal Paradox."

John considered this for a moment and muttered:

"Well, if that's true, then somebody must move the body back at some point. I think we have to risk it."

Against the young knight's protests, Hugo ordered two of his men to rewrap the body and move it to the short tunnel we had seen earlier, which had prepared alcoves already cut into its rock walls.

With picks, Claude and two other men worked to drive three holes deep into the rock at the end of the tunnel. We used picks and straight irons to drive smaller shafts further into the rock. These, we packed with dynamite from one barrel and lit a fuse.

Even from a safe distance we were still almost deafened by the blast. My hearing was particularly affected; I couldn't hear properly for hours after. We approached the blast area nervously. Even as we stepped through the clouds of dust, water wetted our feet and ankles.

"We did it!" one of the knights yelled.

"We did *something*!" John replied.

***

Chapter Five

As the dust cleared, could see through a hole, roughly the height of a child, into an old watercourse which ran perpendicular to our tunnel. It sloped to the right, and a small rivulet gurgled in its bottom, some of the water now spilling into our tunnel.

John led us into the watercourse and then backed out.

"There are torched coming from the left. Put out the torches, and follow me. Quick!"

He ducked back into the watercourse and turned right. He broke into run and we followed him, wading and stumbling against the sides of the narrow channel.

"It must be this way, toward whatever the Romans found," John told me over the echoes from the rushing water.

I was right behind John. We had only waded perhaps fifty feet when we came across an opening on the left and through it the roof of a vast cavern. Our water course was near the top. Below, we both saw a scene of pandemonium; gangs of naked and chained men and women, whipped by the tall guards, vied for space with the salamander-men on tracks between springs and pillars of rock.

John and I dropped down behind the parapet of our watercourse.

"Where do you think they will have Georgina?" John asked me.

"Somewhere safe, well up in that upside-down world of Satan. Who knows how deep in Hell he hides his trinkets."

John turned to the other men and explained;

"At some point, you will find yourself upside down. That's the way it works in here. Gravity is reversed." He paused. "Hm. I'm not relishing this. Ruth must here too, and the Master, Satan, must be here somewhere. If he is interested in us, I guess the game is up. Last time I was here, I couldn't take wolf-form. But Ruth told me that was, because I was vastly outnumbered. Perhaps, together, things will be different."

John closed his eyes and concentrated on something. Moments later, he growled, and I saw his muscles bulging under his kudra.

Some of the others, including Hugo, did the same, but it seemed not all could transform yet. John turned to his men:

"Focus on your deepest anger. Let it flow through your veins. Imagine you are swimming through your anger to a place where light replaces the darkness. If you cannot transform, stay with Hugo. If you need it, his sword will balance the scales. Grandfather Hugo, you come with me. You will lead our support team. Leave two of your men, who can transform, to blow a hole in this wall." Hugo picked two knights. John turned to them. "It might not do much damage, but the flooding will be an increasing distraction. You must hold this escape route for us as long as you can and then get out. Guillaume, you didn't ask for this. There is a Gate which is open at midda- … ."

"I'm Ordo Lupus. It's my duty you're your little crusade."

"Very well. Stay with Hugo. Zosimyache … . Claude, you stay with us. You can resist fire, and you'll need that in here!" John put his hand on my shoulder:

"You come with me too"

I nodded.

"Blow the wall as soon as you can!" John shouted over his shoulder as we leaped over the wall.

There was a small ledge beneath the parapet and below this an angled rock wall. It was steep but had enough handholds for us. Hugo and two men followed us down the wall. I cast the cloak and would only have appeared a shadow at John's side. We took up position behind a huge rock pillar to observe the chaos in front of us.

"Ignore the salamanders, with yellow and black stripes," John told the others. "They don't care about us. What we need are a few of those guard suits!"

"I might be able to get one," I suggested.

"Try."

When a platoon of the strange creatures approached us, I crouched and loped over the track to the quieter of the two tracks to our right. One of the ten-foot, faceless guards leaned against a wall. I hid, discarded my clothes and transformed into dog form. I loped past the guard casually but then turned and tore at the flesh where a face should be. To my horror, it had no effect. The monster picked up his enormous sword and twisted it in its grip, so that he could slash my throat.

"Oh no you don't!" I growled. "That's my move. Thinking of a bear, I found that my enlarged foreleg was able to force his arm back against the wall. I squeezed hard, and the beast dropped his sword, clanging, to the ground. I ripped off its helmet and tore a large piece of his head off. The body slumped to the ground, lifeless. I dragged the body behind a large rock and stripped off the armour. Within moments, I was back at the pillar, and John was trying on the armour. It was far too big for him, he had to discard the leggings, but it had to do.

"The track leads into a long tunnel over there, to the right. Just like that one." I explained, nodding to a vast tunnel to our right.

"We find another and get his too," John said. "I don't think you will need your kudra, my friend. Just your sword."

It didn't take long for another victim to come along.

But things wouldn't be so easy, this time.

A guard marched purposefully out of the tunnel, past the rock, behind which I was concealed. I was in man form now. Claude and John were concealed behind the pillar, with the first body.

Just after the guard passed, I drew my blade and brought it round to strike at his back.

My blade connected but didn't penetrate, because it was parried by a curved blade held by somebody behind me.

"Behind you!" John yelled.

I spun round. Five men in white kudras faced me. One of them held the katana, the curved sword used by Samurai, that was binding my blade. The giant guard also slowly turned round.

Oh, oh! Surrounded!

"Concilium Putus Visum!" John yelled.

"With you!" Claude yelled.

I turned through a full circle, swinging my blade but connecting with nothing. It didn't matter. I was just playing for time to think. The space wasn't confined, we were outnumbered, and Claude was not a good swordsman. Looking at the relaxed stance and blank expressions of our opponents, I knew they would be difficult to beat, especially since I was weary from fighting and 'changing.'

John and I had swords whose steel would be softer than the katanas, but they had long cross-guards and heavy pummels, both of which could be used to good effect. I hoped John would learn from me; although he was proficient, he had nothing like my 2500 years of battle experience. Indeed, experience would be my main advantage. All these thoughts went through my head in a fraction of a second.

"Claude. Take their rear! Strike when you can. Back off!"

Thinking I had already taken advantage of any courtesy the CPV swordsmen might give me, I twisted my sword and brought the flat of the blade up against the katana, using a typical hard bind to force the enemy's blade toward the roof of the tunnel behind him. I wanted to demonstrate my power quickly.

His face revealed no emotion as he stepped back and brought his blade to a passive, vertical position, guarding his face. He was balanced well on his heels.

A good fighter

Not hesitating, I had swung my sword through a long arc to thrust between the second and third men.

As I expected, the two adjacent men stepped back and away, to avoid their companions. This left one group of three to me and two to John, once he had despatched the tall guard. The CPV had already shown a weakness; they were not experience at fighting in a group and crowded each other.

John didn't fail me. Taking advantage of an exposed back, he lined up his sword carefully and drove it through the armpit of the guard will holding the blade with both hands like a spear for accuracy. The guard moaned as the blade went through some vital organ and slowly fell to his knees but not before twisting round to take a swing at his executioner. John stepped away just in time. The huge, pitted blade took a few downy whiskers off of John's teenage face and 'clanged' off a rock on the ground.

I saw this, because I had to turn to get behind the guard of my nearest enemy. Pivoting on my hips I aimed a lateral swing at his hip, catching him off guard. He tried to step away, but my blade drove through his kudra and flesh and was only stopped two inches into his hip bone. He screamed and pulled away from me. Over his falling body stepped the man who had first blocked my thrust to the guard. His eyes glinted with a devout cruelty. At the same time, I felt a hot burning sensation in a long line from my neck, just beneath my ear, to my lower back and heard the clash of two swords behind me.

I felt blood oozing from the long wound, but I was still able to stand.

I had hoped John would have his back to me by now, so that we would not have to worry about hitting each other. Then I felt a back against mine and saw his blade to my left.

"Use your hilt!" I suggested. "Your warning was a bit pointless by the way; behind you!"

My enemy made two swinging cuts, one from my left and one from my right. He wanted to watch my reaction, find the flow of battle and control it. But I too wanted to control it. I used two predictable moves. I parried his first blow by soft binding, absorbing his blow with my blade angled, and following through its path. I used a hard bind on the second to drive against his force, again with an angled blade and use my legs arms and torso to force a strike against his inner arm.

I almost made it. But he was quick, quicker than any I had encountered for many years. Moreover, I could tell now that he was trying to move me into the mouth of the tunnel by stepping back just a little further each time. I didn't know what advantage this could give him, but I feared it.

I had a feel for him now, he played largely by the rules but would take great delight in killing me. I saw a way I could beat him and could waste no time. I was already tiring.

I thrust to his right side, appearing to step forward too far and ending on my toes. As I had wanted, he saw his advantage and stepped to the side to launch his own attack. But to my horror, he switched the sword to his other hand and aimed a very powerful swing at my back. I hadn't anticipated this, so I had to play dirty. I stepped slightly to the right and barged into his side, so that his swing went behind me, thus voiding its power. At the same time, I drove into his waist at his kidneys with the pummel of my hilt and just for good measure, twisted my grip and tore a chunk of his flesh out with my crossguard.

"You don't know who you're fighting," I whispered into his nearby ear, just to frighten him.

But by now, I was half under the tunnel arch, just where I didn't want to be. Something here would give him an advantage and furthermore, my other opponent now had the space he needed to outflank me. It was not a good moment.

His blade was harder than mine. While mine was further blunted, his had lost some of its edge and had nicks along its length. I brought down a hammering blow with the edge of my blade from above his shoulder. He responded with a hard bind which was a mistake. Not only could he not match my power, but he would fear that his sword might break. He abandoned the move, trying to convert it into a soft bind, but this may have dislocated his arm. In any case, he switched back to his other hand and glanced at his blade for damage.

There was indeed a large triangle of steel torn from the edge but his glance was rather stupid. It is never recommended that you use a vertical cut from below. It is difficult to aim and, by most accounts, impossible to achieve much more than a superficial wound, at least in battle terms. But I wanted to be unpredictable, and I had still enough strength left to deal a fatal blow. I hadn't used the move since my foolish youth, but now was a good time to try again. I pretended to thrust for his shins, to which he answered by going for a soft bind to direct my blow to the stone ground.

Nice move.

But I knew he would do that. Quicker than he could think, I moved my blade ahead of his and withdrew it before thrusting directly between his legs and swinging the blade vertically upwards. Both my feet were carefully planted apart, and I even managed to get my second hand to my hilt to apply my full force to the blow. I felt my shoulder muscles almost tearing as the blade struck, and I drove it up through his groin and into his abdominal cavity.

Gore and blood spattered my blade, hands and face and the cruel man had a sudden childlike look of surprise in his eyes. He attempted to stand, but his body gave way. Before he could fall, I had to parry the blow of the second man.

While we fought, I was vaguely aware that mane of the salamander-men passed us. They seemed unconcerned by our fight, even though several of them became collateral damage in the fights.

My last adversary was not in the same class as the second. But I was tired now. My blade's edge would have been rolled in many places, making it almost ineffective. To his first thrust, which he executed correctly by using one hand on the blade, I replied with a parry and then held my own blade in the centre while stepping forward, so I could thrust the crossguard into his face. I missed, but the move put him off. He stepped away and began a lateral swing toward my right side, twisting his hip to apply his full strength.

I could see he hoped this would be the fatal blow. I used a hard bind with the back of my blade to stop the blow but only when his flank was slightly to the left of the axis of my blade. Without hesitating, I continued my own move to thrust with my feet, hands and body in what is called in kenjutsu the Fire and Stone Cut[5]. My blade went into his side between two ribs and continued on to slice through his heart. There was no hope for his life now. He dropped his sword arm, briefly gripped his side, looked at the blood on his hand and smiled.

"That's a lesson for you!" I gasped.

I saw his eyes close and began to turn to John's assistance. I have never made such a mistake before or since. It is well known that a falling man can still strike out and furthermore that a dying animal can be the most dangerous.

From the corner of my eye, I saw the strike come. It was a feeble one by any standard but was aimed at my exposed heart from behind. I had barely enough time to swing my blade and move aside by a few inches. His blade caught mine as his grip released. The blade slid along mine and took my little finger off above the second joint.

There was no time to think about it, no pain yet to scream about. I saw that two of John's opponents were down, but the last was getting the better of my friend.

With a single thrust, holding my blade like a spear, I drove my blade clean through the chest of the man, from behind. I imagine he must have been quite surprised by the steel protruding from his ribs. He dropped his arms to his side and then his whole weight fell upon my blade. I let him fall and used gravity to withdraw the blade.

"That was close!" John gasped. If it hadn't been for Claude and you, I would be finished!"

Claude grinned at me.

"I lost a finger," I announced.

"I didn't do so well either!" John replied. He had a new gash to add to the collection on his face and a nick in one ear. Only Claude was uninjured.

"Soon there won't be much left of you to cut off!" I declared.

I bound my finger as tightly as I could while Claude

and John concealed the bodies.

We headed into the tunnel together. Within only ten feet or so, cart tracks climbed the walls and then continued on the roof.

John led us up the walls, and we continued down the tunnel. Now I could see what the swordsmen had hoped for. If we had been drawn into the tunnel, they would have had its whole circumference to use as a killing floor.

"I think I know where that goes!" John yelled. "Up this ramp." He added, "Now I definitely *know* there is something seriously wrong. The CPV in here can only mean they are serving the Devil now."

A nearby ramp spiralled upwards for hundreds of feet before emerging into a tunnel wide enough for three carts to pass. We turned left and immediately to our left was a narrower staircase. Ahead. In the distance, upside down, we could see the court and the dais where we had fought the Serpent. John led us up the narrow staircase. A short way up the steps became a smooth slope. Steps could be seen on both walls and, further on, upon the ceiling. John ran up the walls and on to the ceiling. We followed and he led us on, to the first landing.

"This must be where you were held!" I yelled over the cacophony of trumpets and bellowing monsters that announced war was breaking out in Hell.

"Hugo!" John yelled. "You and your men hold this landing. We will be back!"

A moment later, there was a loud boom.

"The gunpowder!" Hugo yelled.

John ran on, up the stairs, but I noticed his gait was less steady. Claude and I followed him. The intensity of heat was unbearable, and John's suit burst into flame on the stairs.

"Take it off!" I yelled. Claude stripped too.

"I have to tell you," John said, with his mouth against my ear, "that I cannot feel my leg much past my knee now. And there's something else. Somebody or something, has been trying to get in my head for hours. I have felt it before, in Paris. The Serpents can read minds. I can block them for a while but it's getting worse. Soon they will know we are here!"

We reached the next floor. All round us were vast rooms, filled with writhing couples of both sexes, coming acts of sex and bestiality that I had only seen in pornographic illustrations. All were enveloped in fire and alternately screamed with pain or fear and then moaned with pleasure.

The pattern was much the same as we ascended the levels. It became a dream as we sought for one lonely woman, ourselves now burning like human candles.

"I can hardly see!" John cried.

"We're with you!" I heard myself and Claude reply. I wasn't sure if I was dead or alive. Fearing no human could survive in such a place, I quickly told Claude how he could transform himself into a dog. He concentrated hard, but nothing happened.

On the next floor, we saw bodies, wallowing in muck and filth, watched over and whipped by a demon in the shape of a giant, many-headed dog. The floor after that contained a crazy, never-ending stairway, up which men and women pushed large boulders.

On the fourth floor, prisoners of both sexes hung from chains on the walls, their guts being ripped out in front of their eyes. Limbs were torn off and heads removed, all while the witnesses screamed in agony. I watched one ancient and bearded man's face. His hollow eyes pleaded for release from the eternal agony, but I could do nothing. I turned and followed John, upwards.

"I don't think I can take much more!" I yelled. It was

only John's friendship that bore me on.

I had transformed to wolf-form, and John was now fully changed into a wolf, so huge that he terrified me. I had to look away and, in so doing, I noticed that Claude had finally changed to wolf-form.

Blind leading the blind!

At last, John seemed to sense something. He turned into a corridor and loped along it at a pace I could hardly match. At the end, he smashed a vast door off its hinges and stared into a round chamber.

Claude and both stood behind him, trying to take in the scene, but then Claude swung round, and my eyes followed his gaze. Down the corridor strode a very tall man, black as ebony and as muscular as a statue. He was naked, and his ears extended into small wings, either side of a grinning face, made grotesque by fangs that extended upwards and downward, outside his mouth.

"Hold him for a few moments!" I shouted to Claude.

My friend leaped on the man while John and I ran toward another beast, like the man, but with a long snake-tail instead of legs and wings that encased something on his lap. Seven other such creatures sat on thrones around the circumference of the chamber.

John ripped the wings away from their sockets with incredible strength and screamed:

"No!"

On the mutilated beast's lap, there was a sphere of human flesh. I could make our arms and legs and even a face with its hair, but all were distorted to form a grotesque ball. The face was Georgina's. I knew she must be dead.

"John!" I tried to yell. I don't know if any sound came from my mouth.

Then I saw that the beast was committing coitus with the fleshy sphere, surely the ultimate depravity. The other beasts all groaned with pleasure and revealed their loins. They all, it seemed, had taken their fill of pleasure with the sphere of flesh in a grotesque ball-game.

John grabbed the ball from the beast threw it toward me. It landed just short, but we both saw the face's mouth move:

"John! It's not real! I'm still alive! Don't leave me!" Georgina's mouth said.

I spun to help Claude who was now pinned to the wall by the black figure, who said:

"John! We meet again! It is Chalcathgna. This is how I truly look. Better than you, I might say! My Master is busy but will be here shortly. Shall I kill this one now?"

"No. Take me."

John leaped upon the Chalcathgna and tore at his neck. The black man dropped Claude, who was missing two fingers and a long strip of flesh from his side.

"Take the girl. Down!" I yelled before joining John. I saw Claude grab the ball of flesh in his teeth and head for the stairs from the corner of my eyes.

In Hell, it seemed, the Serpents were actually weaker in their snake form, brought on by sexual activity. But Chalcathgna was strong, very strong. Both John and I tore at his limbs, I being flung against the walls several times before I managed to get my fangs into a vein. But the only effect it had was to make me feel sick. I let go. I saw that John now had his fangs in the beast's neck and Chalcathgna was wailing and thrashing his huge arms around in agony. Each one of his nails grew into a talon, dripping with venom, and he slashed at John's back.

Only John had managed to retain his sword, and I saw it, lying against a wall. I lunged for it, picked it up and brought it down upon the beast's wrist. The blade broke in two but not before Chalcathgna's hand was severed.

Chalcathgna screamed in agony, threw John away from him and retreated, down the corridor.

We turned and saw the other Serpents regaining their senses. Some already had returned to the man-shape of Chalcathgna.

"Talk about stirring up a hornet's nest!" I yelled.

"Let's go!" John suggested.

It was, on the whole, one of John's best suggestions, and I leaped down the stairs after him. Never have I felt more relieved to leave a place, or nightmare.

***

We reached Claude and Georgina where Hugo, Guillaume and the other knight were fighting a rearguard action against fifty of the faceless guards. Even Guillaume was in wolf shape and tearing guards from limb to limb. While they fought, John cradled Georgina, who now looked quite human, though very young, fragile, exhausted and bloody.

"John, she murmured. "There's something I have to tell you!"

"Not now!" he assured her. "Where's Ruth? And the Master? We have to … ."

"No! Listen. There is somebody else you need to save. In the Ring. She walks in the Ring!"

"Even now?" I asked.

"Yes. It never stops. There's time. Ruth will be preparing herself to leave. She needs time."

John considered for a moment, while Georgina kissed his muzzle and peeled away one of his bloody bandages.

"Hugo!" John growled. "Take your men back to the watercourse. Wait ten minutes, and then get out!"

We sped off, John carrying Georgina in his muscular

arms, toward the court in front of the dais. In the long tunnel, Georgina stopped us.

"Not now. Ruth will be there. Wait! Just a minute or two."

After waiting, she told us to go on. Sure enough, the ring of naked girls was still circling while a Serpent writhed in ecstasy with one of them on the red-velvet festooned dais.

Georgina stared at each girl in turn, before pointing to one.

John carried Georgina in his arms while Claude and I followed him. To the girl. I drew her aside and John stood, staring at her. To my surprise, he put Georgina down and swept the girl into his arms, sobbing:

"Annie! Annie! Can it be you?"

"Daddy? Daddy!"

The girl looked too shocked to speak for some moments and then broke into tears. The both enveloped each other in their arms.

I put my paw on John's shoulder and told John:

"We must go! Hugo won't hold out long!"

John, carrying his daughter, Annie, on his back and I, carrying Georgina, followed Claude as ran down the huge tunnel at the end of the court. Toward the end of the tunnel, near where it opened out into the vast cavern where we had first entered, cart tracks led up the walls onto the ceiling and continued on. Water ran along the roof of the tunnel, toward us and then fell in a curtain of water to the floor we were running on. Also, along the roof. A troop of faceless guards rushed toward us, brandishing weapons.

"Keep running!" John hollered, splashing through the runnels of water. "As fast as you can!"

Claude ran straight through the curtain of falling water and then appeared to take off and fly! John, followed him, carrying Annie, and I, after.

Suddenly, my feet left the ground and I felt Georgina and I falling up! I twisted round, so that my feet faced the great lake of water that now filled the underground cave. We flew straight over the heads of the attacking guards. Georgina gripped my fir, painfully tight, but held on. My stomach felt as if it were being churned like milk as we passed through the gravity distortion. That was the only thing that passed through my mind before I had to think where to land.

Claude fell into water, between two floating carts, but John and I both landed on the heads of wading guards. Using their heads like stepping-stones, we leaped from one to the next and onto those of swimming guards toward the rock wall. We both dragged ourselves up the wall and looked back for Claude.

Everywhere we looked salamander-men fought to keep their blank faces above the water while faceless guards bellowed impatient commands. They hardly even noticed us, concerned as they were with their own survival now. Claude quickly lost the will to stay in animal form, and as a normal, if naked, man, he struggled to cross the churning pool.

The last spears from Hugo's knights flew over our heads, keeping the enemy at bay.

But then there was a horrific scream overhead when the first Serpent arrived.

"I knew there was another!" John gasped.

The beast swooped on us just as John, in the lead, clambered out of the water and started the long climb up the rock face. John ducked, and the beast missed him by inches. Not to be denied it tried for Georgina and I. I had to duck under water, but when I emerged, it was to the screams of my friend Claude. The Serpent had him gripped in its jaw and the claws at the joint of his wings and was gaining height. With the effort, it became unaware that it was drifting toward the gallery, high over our heads.

With a howl, Hugo leaped from the broken parapet and landed on the beast's back. The beast juggled Claude in its mouth, crushed his torso and ripped off his head, dropping the bloody corpse into the water next to me.

Oh Claude! Well at least you found your glorious death!

As I struggled up the rocks, I saw Hugo draw the huge, silver sword and thrust it deep into the back of the Serpents neck, just below the skull.

With a howl of first rage, and then blinding pain, the beast shook its head to try and free the blade and sunk toward the water. A second serpent was coming to the aid of the first and swooped on Hugo.

By now, John was at the parapet and Hugo's last two knights, Guillaume and one other, dragged the two survivors over the wall, against the flow of water. Arms extended down to grab me, and I gladly let them take my weight. As I twisted at the end of the human rope, I saw Hugo being lifted off the water in the jaw of the second Serpent.

"Can't nobody help him?" John cried.

But it was too late. Though Hugo struggled to bring the blade to bear on the Serpent's neck, his head was taken into those great jaws and his skull was crushed. Even as he died, Hugo took one last swing at the neck and half-severed it. The beast fell against the rock wall and tumbled to the rocks below, with Hugo's dead body still in its embrace.

The sword clattered to the ground.

John didn't hesitate. He left Annie with Guillaume, who had also changed back to a man, and dived off the rock, into the water. He climbed out and picked up the sword. Dragging this and Hugo's body, he started up the wall.

I leaped down the wall and grabbed Hugo's body from him. Together, to the yells of encouragement from the men, we clambered back to the watercourse. From the corner of my eye, I could see four more Serpents arriving. But we made it just in time.

The last survivors, along with the two we had rescued, headed back up the watercourse, and into a throng of faceless monsters, wearing no armour. Stripped to loincloths, they wielded the oversized axes, maces and swords of the guards, but they could barely swing them in the narrow space.

"Zosimyache!" John cried. "I'm … too tired! We need you!"

"I'm too … bloody tired too!" I cried.

I had let myself slowly become a man again. It was far less tiring. The last thing I wanted now was to try and change to animal form. In fact, I wasn't even sure I could. But I had to try.

I shuffled near to the front of our short line and focused on the shape of a bear. I must have been very weary, because nothing happened, at first.

A mace swung into my face sending me sprawling, with several broken teeth. The anger I felt welling up must have helped me, because I felt myself transform into the biggest, blackest bear I have ever become. I charged into the pack of attackers, smashing through them like a freight-train. My momentum only ran out when I reached the hole through to the quarry.

"Get out!" I growled.

I saw the others struggle through the hole and then backed out behind them. I quickly returned to human form and took Hugo's body from Guillaume. While the other knight carried the silver sword, we ran after Guillaume, who had memorised every twist and turn of the tunnels. We ran until we could hear our pursuers no longer.

***

We were all weary to the bones. We fell to our knees in the limestone dust, heaving for air. John was in the worst condition and lay prostrate.

"I thought you would never come!" gasped Guillaume.

"Put something on the women," John murmured. The second knight and I searched for something for the women to wear. In the large cavern, we found some discarded sacking which we tied together. We were both too weary to talk. We could hear voices near the entrance to the quarry, so we didn't loiter. When we returned, John was standing up, but even then, he stubbed his numb foot on a rock and grimaced.

"Can't feel it!" he explained to the knight, who was little more than a boy. "What's your name?"

"Baldwin de Raysor."

We wrapped the sacking around the naked women, and Georgina began to bind John's wounds. Annie sat against the wall, shaking uncontrollably.

Shock.

"Baldwin." John continued. "Are you badly hurt? You don't seem as bad as us two."

It was true. John and I looked like ghouls.

"Not too bad," Baldwin answered. He held up his arm to show a deep slash to his forearm muscle.

"So many dead!" John muttered. He seemed to hesitate for a moment and then added, "No! We must go on! We must succeed. Hugo sacrificed himself for us."

"He killed two, same as you!" I replied. "And I have none!"

"You don't want to. They are *terrible*!" John retorted.

"For Claude," I replied.

"Baldwin. We need water, clothes, and we need to know what's happening out there … ."

Georgina had been quietly working away at John's wounds with torn off strips of Baldwin's tunic until now. She touched John's hand lightly before whispering:

"Jean. I need to tell you something. I have been thinking and have come to a decision. I need your help and you need my help. There is something that must be done."

"Go on Georgina. Speak up, so we can all hear. We are *all* going to live or die, together.

"Not with that freak here!" Georgina spat.

I must admit, it did seem strange to hear a sixteen-year old woman talking to a sixteen-year old man as a mature, ex-couple. Georgina continued:

"She has been wrapped up tight with Satan for far longer than *I* have!"

"You have hardly earned our trust either!" John countered.

"I think she is asleep anyway," whispered Guillaume.

"Good. Talk," John told Georgina. "We don't have much time."

But Georgina wasn't so easily reassured. She walked over to the sleeping form of Annie and bent down.

"Freak! Wake up!" she whispered in the girl's ear. Annie didn't stir. Georgina came back and sat down, facing John.

"I'm not even sure she's real myself," John explained. "How could she possibly survive so long in Hell? I have wondered if it's another trick!"

"No trick," Georgina replied. "As she will tell you, Satan has been keeping her as his plaything. Not his favourite though. That was me until you came along, and another girl replaced me. She survived for so long, because she is neither from Heaven or Hell. She is a new creation by *God*! A freak! But we don't have time for that now. I told you about the twelve people on Earth; that they are real, the rest are not. I didn't tell you that things have changed lately. One of those twelve has been murdered. By another. It upsets the balance."

When the Devil went to Hell he took one twelfth of the souls with bodies with him, but these souls kept switching with those in Heaven until God could not distinguish good souls from bad and so didn't know who to exclude from Heaven any more. So he created Earth where he could send all the souls and begin to decide who should be in Heaven and who in Hell. He created a reflection of Heaven and Hell which was Earth."

This is where the twelve live and watch over the growth of the beings who inhabit either Heaven or Hell. But the ratio of evil to good has always been one to six, because of the power of Satan. The murder took place in 1881, and now the balance is disturbed. It will remain so until a ceremony is carried out on top of Cologne Cathedral that same year, 1881."

"Why there?" John asked.

"Because the Angels carry a code inside them. They don't have DNA, they have the Synchronicity Code. It carries a pattern for the flow of time, of events. Each Angel is charged with making sure certain aspect of Earth's development occur; spiritual, cultural, industrial even."

I must have smiled or grunted, because John looked at me and Georgina stopped speaking. I smiled and said:

"It was as I thought."

"Um. In the eventuality that an Angel was killed," Georgina continued, "God coded in a plan to constantly

build higher and higher religious structures; the closer
to God, the easier for the ceremony to take place. In
1881, Cologne is the highest. For the balance to be
restored, the Angel's body must be placed in a container
at the top of the tower for a full solar day. That day will
be 9 April, and the process will be complete at
midnight. A special rite takes place in the building
below involving the twelve Angels and a helper each at
the begging of those twenty-four hours. They must all
attend for it to work. It will be the first time they have
all been together on Earth. If it works, a barrier or field
will be placed around the body which none can
penetrate, not even the Angels. At least that was what
was thought until Annie came along. It seems that the
field can be penetrated by one who is neither good nor
evil, an exact balance, or perhaps one who is neither
from Hell of Heaven. Annie is such a person. Satan's
plan was to use her to penetrate the field and destroy
the body, thus permanently upsetting the balance of
good and evil in his favour. There is a backup plan if
this doesn't work; um, the construction of Cologne
Cathedral was halted for 400 years and only restarted in
1842. A huge, medieval crane had been left on the
tower for all that time and was still in place in 1856. If
it can be used to lift a block, it can be swung and the
tower destroyed. It cannot be repaired in time for the
ceremony. Chalcathgna will do it. He is already
preparing to leave. The Master has already left!"

"Without Annie?"

"There is another now. Satan has been working on
her. She is neither good nor evil. But she is the creation
of Satan. It is not certain she will pass through the field.
She is the assistant that the Master has taken. There is
not much time. Today is the last day the Gate is open."

"What is the name of Satan's creation?" I asked
Georgina.

"Violet Bell."

"But to what year does the Gate go?" John asked.

"1856!"

John smiled. Of course. Now I know who builds the Gates. This is a lot to take in. But I still don't understand how Annie could survive! There was a DNA sample from the dead Serpent at Beauvais which matched a sample taken from her clothes when she was murdered in Nevers!"

"I would love to lie to you Jean!" Georgina replied. "But I can't. It was planted. I was involved. The body was, ow you say, a plant? Of course, the sample matched. Chalcathgna killed her and crushed her, just to trick you."

"Oh God! I wish Rose had lived longer. We have to move fast. Let me think.

"Wait John! Why should we trust her? Why is she helping us *now*?" I interjected.

"Yes. Good question," he replied. "Georgina?"

"I don't know. Because I love you John. Because the balance has been upset."

For a long while, John stared into her eyes. Then he answered me:

"I think she is telling the truth. Mostly. Now I have to think. While I think, Guillaume and Baldwin, find water, food and clothes. And find out as best you can what time it is. Outside, I have no doubt the Serpents will be waiting for us, but we have to reach the Gate. There's just a chance they're attacks will not be so coordinated with Chalcathgna wounded and Satan gone! Don't go far! If you cannot find anything, come back quickly!"

With his men sent out, John seemed even wearier. After we dressed, he sat with his head upon his knees and withdrew into himself. I noticed that his leg, below the knee, was as black of that of Chalcathgna. Georgina and I watched each other warily while I stood guard over Annie. I didn't know what to make of her. Could she be *that* special? Was the canny and tricky Georgina telling the truth? I had my doubts. I suspected another trap, and my missing finger ached terribly. What I would have given for a warm bed, a glass of blood and a friendly female body.

It wasn't long before the two knights returned, carrying two gourds of water, some kudras bread, cheese and pomegranates.

"It was all we could find," Baldwin explained.

"And not easy!" added Guillaume. "We had to, de facto, borrow it.

"And the time?" John said, raising his head.

"You know what time is here!" Guillaume replied. With no sun, nobody seems sure. A senior Jew, returning from the Temple told me it was within an hour of midday."

"Looking at you John, I think you have to leave now," I added. "You will be a boy in less time than that!"

"Yes. Eat and drink everyone. I have decided what to do."

While we ate, John told us his plan:

"When I came here, my only plan was to rescue Georgina and take her back to the 20th Century. Now, I see that I can't do that. But I have found Annie, something I never dreamed of. I want both to be safe, as safe as possible. Zosimyache, am I right that you can take Annie back to the 20th Century, back to her family and friends?"

"I would say no, but if she is so special, possibly. We can try."

"And would you do it? I don't want you drinking her dry of blood!"

"John!" I protested. "Of course. You can trust me. I

need blood, but I can get it elsewhere. In this world, there is always blood spilled."

"Good. Then you go first. If it works, then I will go with the others to stop this crane being toppled. I will need all the help I can get! Where will you do it?"

"Outside the City is best. We will need to run. I hope she can run fast!"

"She was fast at school. I don't know any more. She is a *woman*, a middle-age woman inside now. Zosimyache, you heard everything Georgina told us. If I succeed, you have to stop Satan disrupting this ceremony. You must win! You wanted to do some great act. This will be it! I am sure then that you will deserve Jesus's blessing."

"I will do my best," I replied.

"And what of me?" Georgina replied. "Do I get absolution?

"We met Jesus!" John replied. Georgina's beautiful cinnamon eyes opened wide. "He spoke of you. He said you had some great destiny to fulfil too." I didn't point out that Jesus had not used the word 'great.' Georgina was silent.

We finished eating and drinking.

"Five minutes and then we go," John announced. "I need five minutes with my daughter. Zosimyache, take Georgina to the embalmed body. It may be Jesus after all. Behind the body, you will find my book. Keep it with you, and make sure Annie gets it at the end.

I led Georgina to the body and retrieved the book from John's hiding place. To my surprise, Georgina dropped to her knees in front of the body and began fervently to pray.

I left her to it and withdrew to read what John had written so far. This was when I found out how he had found Georgina. I only know what he said to Annie in those five minutes because of a note he scribbled in it later. The note read:

> Spoke to Annie alone for the first time. I was scared. Was she my daughter? Was she the same person? It turned out, nothing had changed. She cried when I held her.
>
> "Daddy, I have been so long without anybody to love or love me. What happened?"
>
> "You were in Hell. Satan took you, because you are so special. He also wanted to tempt me."
>
> I told her that her mother had died but that we had to separate. She had to go with Zosimyache and help him defeat Satan. After that she would be able to go to our old house in Nevers and contact our family. As I spoke, Annie gripped me harder and harder, and her tears began to soak the shoulder of my kudra. I wanted to stop speaking, but I couldn't. "Time to go," I told her.
>
> "Daddy! No!"
>
> I had to wrench her arms away. This will probably be my last entry.

I closed the journal after reading the part about finding Georgina and took the young witch back to the others. On our way out of the quarry, John took his daughter to look at the embalmed body for a few moments. It was a poignant moment for me; watching such a glorious fighter holding the hand of his long-lost daughter and looking at what could be the body of Christ.

***

"Let's go!" John said at the quarry entrance.

We ran as fast as the slowest could manage, toward the Damascus Gate, in the north wall of the City. But it was clear John couldn't move fast, and Annie was too weak.

"We have to split up," John announced. "Zosimyache, you carry on. We're not far from the Gate. The rest of us will go south and create a diversion. Good luck!"

He spun round. I protested, but he was already heading into the night. That was when the first of the Serpents spotted us.

"Through the Gate!" I yelled, pushing Annie forward. "Wait for me outside." I saw Annie making for the gate.

The Serpent swooped down, extending its short talons and large jaw toward my head. I ducked and ran into a narrow alleyway. I was safe however I could not stay there. I climbed the wall, using some plaster decoration for footholds, until I reached the first storey roof. I heard the Serpent's hiss and leaped toward the edge of the tiles. But it had already swooped away.

Horrified, I watched the serpent swoop on Annie!

"Not her! Me!" I yelled, but of course the Serpent was more human than animal; it knew what it wanted.

A man drew his sword and rushed to Annie's defence but was cut down instantly, his head torn from his body. Annie picked up the sword and planted her feet apart, as would any experienced swordsman.

I watched, mouth open, while the Serpent swooped again, and Annie thrust the blade into its wing, ripping a long slit through its leathery surface and an artery.

"That's it!" I whispered.

Angered by unexpected resistance, the beast struck out at me as it passed, trying to gain height. It was too low. I leaped upon its 'shoulders,' just ahead of its great red wings, and clung on while it tried to climb. The slice in its wing impeded its lift severely, and the beast seemed absorbed in its own efforts to save itself. Drawing a sword given to me by Guillaume, I reached around the Serpent's neck.

It knew what I intended and rolled onto its back. Of course, I had to abandon my attempt to slice through its neck or fall off. I could feel its heat burning through my flesh.

The beast executed a half loop and then rolled out on top before diving toward a wide arch.

Has to be now!

Again, I endeavoured to reach around its neck with my blade, but I kept slipping as the beast rolled this way and that. There was nothing for it. I hacked at its wing muscle, and it turned its head to snap at its attacker.

Quicker than it could react, I changed my aim and brought the blade down upon its face. One of its blood-red eyes was destroyed, the other damaged too badly for it to see. We crashed into the ground just beneath the arch, scattering people like skittles.

The beast rolled over me, forcing the air from my lungs, but when we came to a halt in the dust, I was surprised to find myself alive. I stepped off the wrecked and flailing body and ran back toward the Damascus Gate.

Annie was not far beyond. I could see her waving at me, but the guards on the Gate were not going to let me through after the commission in the air. I cast the cloak and dodged between merchants and camels in the mouth of the Gate's tunnel.

The Roman guards were still searching inside the City for me when I grabbed Annie and ran into a grove of olives.

"There's one up there!" she cried. "It's seen me. It

came down and tried to grab me but missed.

"Take my hand. Fortunately, I have seen Cologne Cathedral, but it was a long time ago. Do you know it?"

"Only from photographs at school. I remember it has two spires … ."

"Good! Focus on that. They have a lattice stonework, all the way to the top with a shape like an onion on top, like the Russian Orthodox churches."

"Ha! I never expected a vampire to be funny! Are you going to drink my blood?"

"No. Focus on an image of the Cathedral and run. You will feel a tugging if we don't see the same thing. Hang on tight. My image will be the stronger. Run!"

Together, we ran, but it was not fast enough. Just before we entered into the long, dark tunnel that marks a passage through time, a Serpent descended upon us. I hefted my sword and grabbed it by the end of the blade. Swinging it like a dagger, I launched it up and over our heads. I saw the blade strike the Serpent between the wings an instant before 1st Century Jerusalem was blotted out.

***

I was only told what happened to John later. They passed under the viaduct before the largest Serpent dared to dive on them. The night was filled with the screams of terrified citizens.

"Creatures from Hell! The end of the World!" were the cries that went up.

John used the chaos, keeping to the crowds of panicked people, until they reached Herod's Theatre. The structure was six storeys high, and John decided it offered the best hope of destroying the Serpents. It was closed, but it didn't take much effort for John, now half in his wolf form, to force them open. With the silver sword, he charged to the roof while Georgina and

Guillaume acted as bait on the second floor and Baldwin waited on the third.

"Only three left!" Guillaume assured the young witch.

Two of the beasts came down for the easy kill, swooping almost to the stage before Baldwin slashed one of their number's wings. The beast turned on him. He fought bitterly until the end. When the beast fell on his seemingly dead body, the young knight managed what many more experienced swordsmen could never manage and thrust straight up, piercing whatever the beast had for a heart.

Realising their mistake, the last two beasts gained height, seeking John. That was their second mistake.

John leaped upon the back of the first beast to rise alongside him. With the great sword of his uncle, he made the sacrifice for which it was made. Just one touch of the metal on its writhing flesh, made from that of a thousand dead souls, caused it to scream in agony. It fought for height, clearing the Theatre, but then the blade went deep inside its flesh. The beast seemed to crumple in mid-air, spiralling down in the night to crash on a roof nearby. John stepped out of the wreckage, dazed. But he couldn't wait long.

Some of the last remnant of the CPV, four swordsmen, climbed to the roof and surrounded him. For a few moments, the flashes of the first moonlight in days was seen, reflecting off blades as they fought. John used his sword with the gilt handle now. Trapped, he leaped down to a lower roof and sped off to the south.

As it was told to me, John was tiring and needed a good killing ground for one. He found it in King David's Tomb. The obelisk-like building rose four storeys into the sky.

The Concilium Putus Visum assassins attempted to

corner John, on the first floor and then the second, while the last Serpent circled above. But John was too powerful and quick for them. Leaping from balustrade to platform, ever higher, he engaged them and despatched the first, then the second.

"You can't get away," one of the assassins hissed. "We have come to take you go God!"

"I can't stay," John replied. "And anyway, you serve Satan now. Didn't you know?"

The assassin drew his scimitar down his forearm, drawing a long line of blood.

"I write the end of your life story on this stone plinth with my blood," the hooded man cried. "It has always been the way of the Concilium Putus Visum."

They engaged. Who knows whether John was the quicker, the most desperate or the most skilled? But the assassin fell to his death on the dirt below with his chest open from heart to navel, a fitting end for a bloody story writer.

John leaped onto the balustrade and tensed himself. He launched himself ten feet into the air and caught the post of a railing on the top floor. A pillared arcade ran around the square tower, and John strode behind the arcades, watching for the Serpent, while staying beyond its reach.

The last assassin was brought to him in the talons of the Serpent.

"Fight!" the beast hissed to him.

The last man was the fastest and wariest. That kept him alive a long time. They fought around the pillars, both using them for defence and then to launch surprise attacks. But John was tiring, and finally the man had him caught on the precipitous corner of the floor.

The man looked tense. He drove his blade toward John's heart and kicked with his feet when John used a soft bind. This left him off-balance, so when John kicked his shin, the man grabbed the pillar to stop him falling into space. In an instant, John's blade took off one of his hands, and the man began to fall.

The Serpent dived to catch the man, and John leaped upon its back, forcing it to let the man fall to his death.

"You'll have to fight me after all," John shouted into the beast's ear. "There's always one cautious one."

The beast fought for height and tried to shake off its attacker. Unable to do this, it landed on the pinnacle of the tower and rolled over. John threw down both swords.

"I don't need them anymore!" he yelled. Taking on full wolf form, he expanded almost to the same size as the beast. Rolling around the pinnacle, they bit and chewed at each other. The Serpent almost had its fangs around John's chest when John drove his own poisonous fangs deep into the back of the Serpents neck. The purchase was enough to ease the Serpent away from his chest, and the poison flowed into its hellish veins. John held on while the beast flailed desperately. Eventually, it struggles ceased, and it was left wrapped over the pinnacle like a torn black cloth.

John hardly knew how he had got there. He leaped over the edge and swung, so that he could jump to the top floor. From there, he began to revert to the shape of a man as his passion wore off. By the time he reached the ground, he was running like any wounded man would, slowly. He reached the Theatre and found Georgina kneeling beside a gasping Guillaume. A sword protruded from his gut, and he had another deep wound to his shoulder. Two assassins lay dead at his feet.

"John! A little late, as usual!" Guillaume murmured. Blood dribbled from his mouth when he spoke. "At least the woman is safe! You better go. I'm finished. This is, de facto, not a bad place to die though. Look!"

John turned to look where Guillaume's enfeebled finger was pointing. On the eastern horizon, a piercing beam of light burst from the cloud and bathed the stone pillars around them in a golden light.

"It looks like it's all over here!" Guillaume whispered and slumped forward.

"Come on!" John told Georgina. Together, they ran through the City, out through the Water Gate and on to the Mount of Olives. It didn't take John long to find the Time Gate. Everyone in Jerusalem was rejoicing at the return of light. Above them the sun even appeared, just as John and Georgina stepped through the white beam of the Gate.

***

Chapter Six

I felt Annie's tug on my wrists as we passed through time, a sign that her vision of the Cathedral was different to mine. I held on tight, and we came to a halt in a courtyard I had remembered, north of Burgmauer, the main street that runs alongside the Cathedral and east to the river Rhine, 300 metres away.

It was noticeably cooler that Jerusalem, even cold, but the first thing I did, after I saw that Annie was alive, was glance up at the Cathedral.

It looked just as I remembered; unfeasibly tall and giving me vertigo when I looked up at its stony edifice. But scaffolding on a nearby house obscured the south-eastern tower, where the crane had been and where the spire should now be complete. I stooped to my ward:

"You really *are* special!" I told Annie. "Maybe Georgina wasn't lying after all."

"People are watching us! That woman is screaming!" Annie replied.

It was true. Around us, a crowd was gathering.

"It's our clothes," I reassured her.

My German is not great, but even I could tell that they were shouting things like, "They came out of the air!" and, "We saw them!"

I glanced at the Cathedral from my kneeling position, but a man's head obscured the tower this time.

Damn!

"We have to go," I told Annie.

"I'm exhausted. Just wait a moment! A pint of *blood* would do be good!"

"You've had plenty of victims!"

"But not enough time to drink. Let's go!"

I gripped her firmly by the elbow and headed into the crowd, pushing people out of the way.

"Thanks!" I said. "For earlier. The swordplay; you

almost had that Serpent. Where did you learn your sword skills?"

"I saw a lot of swordplay in captivity. You pick things up. There's no way I am letting them take me back!"

It was some time before we found a quiet street where we could catch our breath.

"What date is it?" I asked a man. He shook his head and walked briskly away.

"We need to change our clothes! Only one way. We need a suitable sized couple."

We had to wait nearly fifteen minutes, at the gate of a house with the lights out, until we saw them. A tall gentleman in a top hat and tails led a slender blonde woman, who was wearing a typical blue 19th Century dress. They appeared to be talking amiably as they walked.

"They will come past this gate, any moment," I told Annie. "Distract the man."

"I?"

I had already torn my kudra into six long strips, concealed myself and cast the cloak. Annie spoke to the man in English. He didn't understand, but as soon as he had his back to me, I put my hand over his mouth and pulled him back into the house's garden.

The woman started to scream, so Annie had to put *her* hand over her mouth. Shifting slightly into the shape of a wolf, I pinned the man against a wall while I reached out and dragged the woman into the garden.

While I applied considerable force, with my hands over their mouths to stop them screaming, Annie picked up a strip of cloth. Trying to sound as menacing as I could, I growled:

"If you want to live, do exactly as I say! Don't make a sound when I let go."

Annie quickly gagged the woman, then the man.

"Take off your clothes now!" I told the man.

When he had stripped to his long-johns, Annie bound his feet, then his hands.

"Take off your clothes," I told the woman.

The woman stripped to her chemise while Annie put on the blue dress and bodice.

When we were both dressed, I dragged both bound prisoners to a shed where I concealed them.

We walked briskly away and found our way back to one of the main streets. I asked another man the time.

"1895 of course!"

When he had gone, I spun to face Annie and told her the bad news:

"It's 1895! We're in the wrong year!"

***

In 1856, John had already stepped out of the Gate with Georgina, in a leafy garden, and was rushing toward the Cathedral. I had a detailed account of what happened later:

"So what were those salamander-men I saw in Hell?" John asked.

Georgina used her limited German to ask for directions to the Cathedral.

"They're the first children of Eve. Not much, are they?"

"I suppose not. Listen Georgina, I feel awkward with you, a distance I know there has been a lot of water under the bridge, but can we be friends now?"

John reached out for Georgina's hand and touched it. She withdrew it.

"Oh John! *Why* do you *care* about me?"

"Because you love me?"

"And I guess I *love* you, because you love me."

She reached out and touched his hand.

"Look at us!" John exclaimed. "We both look like

teenage lovers! We both look great! Ha!"

"*I* look great. You look like a mummy that has escepped!"

John raised her hand and kissed it. They were still holding hands when they turned a corner and saw Cologne Cathedral.

"Wow!" Georgina exclaimed. "Are we going to climb *that*?"

The Cathedral rose like a grey stone mountain, toward Heaven but was truncated well beneath the base of the two spires. Only the roof above the nave seemed complete.

"Takes your breath away, doesn't it? Still unfinished. I can see the old crane up there!"

"I hope you're not scared of heights!" Georgina replied.

"Yes, I forgot to ask Zosimyache that! For him and Annie it will be worse. She isn't scared of heights, but … it will be bloody high!"

"Shouldn't we first do something about our clothes?"

"No time. Look!"

John pointed to the sky. It was just after noon on a sunny day, but high above, the familiar vortex of dark cloud was just beginning to gather.

"Chalcathgna must already be here!" Georgina declared.

"But he's wounded!"

"He will have healed himself by now."

"Right."

A church service was in full-swing at the Cathedral when they arrived at the southern transept entrance. Two burly clergymen raised their eyebrows and then their bejewelled fingers at the approaching strangers.

"He is sick! And we have come from Jerusalem!" Georgina pleaded in her best German.

The two men conferred briefly before giving way reluctantly.

"We're in!" John muttered, though I don't feel quite as able as when I entered Beauvais. I can hardly feel anything below my hip. How much time do I have?"

They turned left and headed past a congregation of at least a thousand people, toward the south-eastern corner of the giant building. The strains of the organ and a vast choir reverberated, echoing, around the inside of the vast building. The vault seemed to hang in space, far above them, making Georgina dizzy when she craned her neck.

"Who knows? A normal person wouldn't have lasted long. A Wolf Angel? Who knows? Maybe a few more hours John. I wish there was something I could do, but I don't seem to have any of my former powers. God, I don't know if I am over sixteen. Perhaps I will die too!"

"Perhaps baby. But you don't seem to be in pain or losing any physical strength. You won't be able to stay here long though; you will still get younger, slowly, but still younger. Maybe a few weeks. Will you find a Gate in time?"

"Don't worry about me. You saved me. I will be fine."

Underneath the southeast tower, there was a vast network of scaffolding. Most of the wood looked ancient but some had been freshly cut, and giant hoists were even now lifting blocks of stone weight a few tons, up into the tower.

"I wonder if that old crane is lifting them?" John speculated.

"We can't just climb up, can *we*?"

"I don't know. There is probably another way. Most of these Cathedrals have a stairwell, built into the walls. It should lead all the way to the top. The question is, where is the damned thing? It could be anywhere!"

After half an hour of fruitless searching, John led Georgina back to the plaza outside the entrance.

"I saw scaffolding on the side of the transept. It looked easier to climb."

"You must be joking! In this wind?"

It was beginning to rain lightly, and the falling drops were accompanied by the first gusts of a storm.

"Damn! We *have* to bloody well find a way up that tower soon!"

"Hey there!" a pile of dirty rags, piled against the Cathedral wall, croaked in heavily German-accented English. "You want to know the way up the tower? I can tell you." A face, with missing teeth and a faded spider-web tattoo around one eye, appeared out of the rags.

"Okay old man. But we have no money!"

"No, but I can see you're not common folk. I have sailed around the world five times, and I never saw anybody who talked like you. Come close."

Georgina stared into the rheumy eyes.

"Not you, pretty lady. Him!"

John took Georgina's place.

"Nein! You're never the age you look. I don't know who you both are, but say a prayer for me, to walk again, when you get to the top, and I'll show you the way. Carry me."

"Don't I know you?" John asked.

"No, but we *may* have met. Sometimes I am known as Mara."

"Mara bar Serapion! Are you the Angel of Death?"

"Ha! Ha! Funny. Do I look like an Angel? Pick me up!"

"Stand up. I am unable to bend."

"John hoisted the beggar onto his back and exclaimed:

"You're as light as a feather old man!"

"Through this gate, into the timber yard. Over there. That shed. Behind it is a stairwell with a locked gate."

"Alright."

"But you need the key for the gate. They keep one inside the shed. Easy to break into."

John responded to the man's squeezing of his shoulder by walking to the shed window.

"There! See it? The big iron key with the leaf design. On the rack?"

"I see it!"

"Good. Now put me back where you found me. I don't want trouble. You know, some say the clouds gathering are, because they build too high! They have been waiting for this day, some all their lifetime! Some say we have tempted the Devil! But I see the workmen coming down alive every day. I know it's not true. Nevertheless, some of the builders say it affects you, being so high."

John returned the beggar to his seated position against the Cathedral wall. The old man croaked:

"Come close."

John crouched down, and the old man whispered in his ear:

"Have you ever felt close to discovering a deeper truth about the way things work, close to being a different *you*?"

John had to think, before replying:

"Perhaps."

"Ha! Ha! And it was a door you wanted to step through, but you couldn't?"

"What are you saying? I don't have time for *this*!"

"Ah! All I will say is that there's a heavy price to pay for entry. But you have paid such a high price already. Go on! Go on!"

John straightened and led Georgina toward the shed.

"Remember to pray for me!" the old man called out.

"What did he say to you?" Georgina asked.

John told her, and her eyes widened with fear.

"Come on!" he told her.

John smashed the shed window and grabbed the key. The key turned the lock in the gate, and they were in.

John stumbled down a short flight of steps and led Georgina along a ribbed tunnel, through the mighty foundations of the Cathedral. They were both too weary to talk. They reached a spiral staircase, just wide enough for two and started up. The dim daylight, streaming through narrow slot-windows placed at very full turn, lit the way for them. Georgina began to count.

"Sorry!" she explained. "Habit!"

"I need to stop," John said after 250 steps. He sat down, gasping for breath. Georgina sat beside him and cradled his head against her shoulder.

"It's a good job it's bloody cold, or I would be dying of thirst," he said after five minutes. "As it is, I could do with a drink. Let's go!"

After 290 steps, they emerged into the belfry.

They traversed around the belfry, before continuing up yet more steps. Now, Georgina was practically dragging John's crippled body up the steps.

"Come on John. I can't drag you much further."

"How many?" he gasped.

"I lost count at 350,"

"We have to get there!"

"Wait. Somebody's coming!"

Down the stairs stumbled a panic-stricken troop of builders. Georgina, and John clung to the steps while they passed.

"Satan!" some of the men screamed.

"Der Teufel!" others screamed.

"You don't have to translate," John gasped. "Chalcathgna!"

"You can't possibly fight him like this John!"

"And give up my one-way ticket to Heaven? Just get me up there!"

"I see the top! At least, I see daylight! Just a few more steps!"

With two more turns of the staircase, they emerged into a confusing world of wood scaffolding and giant stone blocks, cut into crazy shapes.

Below them The Rhine still twinkled greyly, its surface whipped to wavelets by the gales of wind while a few yellow lights flickered in windows and on street pavements. Almost all other light had been blotted out by the black vortex of clouds, now sweeping round the Cathedral.

But John's eyes were drawn to the giant medieval crane, whose four-sided, taping bulk, topped with a shorter cylindrical tower, sat at the centre of a vast wooden platform. The crane[6] itself resembled a giant, squared-off pillbox, fifty feet high, topped by a long cylinder from which a fifty-foot jib extended. Spaced evenly around the edge of the platform were four smaller steam cranes, all unoccupied.

Chalcathgna had ripped the medieval crane's door from its hinges and torn away the casing in his haste to get his huge bulk inside. John caught a glimpse of the giant, black, man-shaped demon before it disappeared. Moments later, the crane hoist began to lift a giant block of stone and then began to swing. On top of the block of stone was a corpse, a man with his hands still close to the hook. As the block swung, the body slipped off crashed into the edge of the platform and fell into space.

"John! Come back! Please! There's something I must tell you!" Georgina yelled. But John didn't hear her. By now, the wind was howling and whipping around them. Georgina began to cry, but John staggered on. Halfway across the wooden platform, he was thrown off his feet by the first impact of the crane's load on one of the Cathedral tower's mighty wall blocks.

The whole tower shook and swayed sickeningly as the stone block, weighing seven tons fell away from the wall and crashed to the ground, far below. John struggled to his feet and almost reached the crane housing when the crane's load crashed into something else; this time a pile of blocks, ready to be used. Each weighed at least four tons and they were sent flying like skittles. One crashed through the edge of the wooden platform falling into the Cathedral interior.

"Chalcathgna!" John gasped, when he reached the torn doorway.

"I knew you would come!" the beast's voice boomed.

***

"But I don't see the problem, even if we are in the wrong year?" Annie said to me, in 1881 Cologne. "Can't we just time-travel again?"

"It's not so simple! I can't understand why we went wrong. Wait! Let me think!" While Annie waited pensively, I paced up and down. "Of course! So stupid! I forgot to tell you the date! Ha! Ha! 9 April, 1881. I normally focus on an image and date, but I have done it so often, I forgot to tell you. I felt you tugging, but I thought it was just your inexperience."

"What do you mean; tugging?

I grabbed Annie's hand and led her back toward the street corner, where we had first arrived.

"Never mind. I need to be sure. I don't have the energy for more than one further attempt."

When we arrived at the street corner, I swung to face the Cathedral. I could see the completed south eastern spire against the starry night sky.

"Looks fine," I muttered to myself. "But that means nothing. If John failed, it still might have been completed by now. We won't know if he succeeded until we get there in 1881. I need to be sure of this. This tenement block looks new. I remember it, but perhaps it wasn't here in 1881. Maybe that is distracting me."

"What is the problem," Annie whispered.

"Excuse me!" I yelled at a man, smoking a pipe at a window. "Was this view of the Cathedral the same in 1881 as it is now? Was this building here then?"

"Surely, no! It was built since then. I don't remember exactly when. I know the owner. Do you want speak to him?"

"No. Thank you."

I held Annie's hand.

"Damn!" I whispered. I only came here after this date. I was just passing through and stood on this street corner when I looked at the Cathedral. That building was there but *not* in 1881. It may stop me from arriving at the right date. We *have* to get this right! They are closing in on us! We have to get out of here fast!"

"A photograph then? The rich get married in Cathedrals, and there are always photographs of them in the doorway."

"Yes. That's good. Wait."

"Oh, but wait! It won't work, because there probably wasn't a wedding on the ninth!"

"Yes. We might have to arrive early, but that drastically reduces my chance of keeping you alive. They will be watching everything in the City. Let me ask! Excuse me?"

"Yes," the man with the pipe replied.

"What is the main newspaper here?"

"There are several, but most read the Gazette."

"Thank you. Do you know where the offices are?"

"No. I am very sorry."

"Come on Annie. We have to find the offices."

"They will be closed … ."

"True. Yet another problem as well as the fact that we now have two tails. You know, John, your father, as good as told me that his life was blighted by bad luck, that he though the Devil intervened to make events swing in his favour. I have a feeling that's what happening to us now. Ever since we left Jerusalem, I have had that feeling. *Nothing* is going our way! Besides, we are being followed. That *proves* somebody intended us to come here. This is only a killing ground, well away from the action."

In the centre of the City, we grabbed a much-needed meal in a tavern. I needed blood but had to make do with a rare steak. It took us a whole hour to find the Gazette offices, but I felt much stronger. I forced the lock door open with ease.

"What are we looking for?" Annie asked, holding a candle

"Large drawers with dates. All newspapers keep back copies."

"I think I've found them then!"

"1881!"

"I know. I have it. April first, third, eighth. *Ninth*!"

"Anything?"

"No. I will backtrack. How good is your German?"

"Only passable."

"What is German for 'Weddings?'"

"'Hochzeiten' or Marriages, 'Ehen.' Here, let me look."

I hurriedly leafed through the pages until I found the section, headed 'Ehen.' There was no photograph of the Cathedral.

After ten minutes of furious searching, Annie shouted triumphantly:

"Got one! 1 April! Look!"

I thought I heard something moving just outside.

"Keep your voice down!" I hissed.

"Oh, but it's too grainy!"

"Let me look. Hm. It would be great. Look, it shows some market stalls. These are very specific. They never last long without changing. It will have to do. We are losing time. Look, it has the credit: Photographer; Johanne Krantz. There will be smaller drawers here with his originals or at least an address. Search!"

There was a smaller chest of drawers, containing the originals from photographers but none marked 'J Krantz. He must just license his work. Wait, I heard something again. Find a small drawer or book with a list of addresses. I'll be back.'

I saw the two hooded men, long before they saw me coming. One was half behind a curtain, the other was stepping across the threshold. Both held guns. I tried to cast the cloak to help me and leaped toward the man behind the curtain. He saw me all too easily, so I thrust my foot into his shin, hard, and then turned my attention to the other.

While the first went down, taking the curtain with him, I palmed the second man's gun away from me. He grunted and tried to bring his trailing leg up to kick me.

Not fast enough!

I side-stepped the kick and drove him to the floor. I took hold of his head and broke his neck in a single, hard wrench.

"Son of Satan! Die" said a voice behind me.

Much to my horror, the second man had disentangled himself from the curtain and had pointed his pistol at me. He pulled the trigger.

I felt the bullet graze my arm, even as I dived away from his line of fire.

I am too slow! This is not good!

I had to roll and get behind a counter to avoid the

second shot. The third, fourth and fifth smashed through the oak counter, barely missing me.

This one means business! Clever too. One more shot.

I waited, and he waited.

"Zosimyache! Are you alright!" Annie called out.

"Stay where you are!" I panted.

"All we want is the girl!" the man hissed with an English accent. "Then you can go!"

"Come and take her then!"

"Damned vampire!" I heard him curse. I took a chance and hoped he wasn't using silver bullets. I dragged a chair round and, throwing it ahead of me, dived for the front door.

The answering bullet sailed right past my ear, singeing my hair in the process.

Damn that was close!

Now he would have to reload. I peered round the door jamb and ducked as the gun flew toward me.

"No more bullets then?" I called.

A moment later, he crashed into me, trying to reach the door. I brought him down and cracked his head hard against the stone sill. Blood and brains oozed from his cracked skull.

"Are you still there?" Annie called.

"Yes. Wait!"

Shame to waste a good corpse!

"What are you doing?"

"Never mind. Coming!"

"I thought you would want to know. I found it!"

"Address?" I asked, arriving at her side. I couldn't stop thinking of the dead man's throbbing carotid artery.

"Yes."

"There will be more outside. We'll go out the back."

"You have blood on your shirt. Are you hurt?"

"No. I am very tired though. I need blood. I thought

perhaps you could wait while I drained one of those men?"

"Oh."

The option of a feast vanished for me when we heard the sound of approaching footsteps in the street.

From the second-floor landing window, I could see an escape route; across an outbuilding roof to a high wall.

"We're have to climb down," I told Annie, forcing open the window. Get on my back."

I turned round and transformed my fingertips into talons, to scale walls more easily. Within a few minutes, we had run along a block of roof tops and climbed down to a quiet street. From there, our trip to the photographer's house was uneventful.

"His light's still on. Let's try tact," I said.

"What do you want?" the poor man replied when he saw my face in the gas light. The look of terror when he saw my bruises and bandaged finger told me that he would let me in.

"They're in there," he explained. "All the photographs of the Cathedral I keep in one box, in date order."

"Thank you. We won't keep you long. Don't worry."

He stood in the doorway, watching us nervously while we sorted through the large plate photographs.

My eyes were transfixed on a photograph, not of a wedding, but some kind of parade in front of the Cathedral. A tall woman in a very elegant dress and shawl was descending from a carriage. Her face was very familiar.

"What is this?" I asked, beckoning over the photographer.

"Ah! A private service. The exact date escapes me, but I think it was 1881. On the back!"

I turned over the photograph and read the date on the

back; 9 April 1881.

"It's Ruth!" I told Annie.

"Let me see. Yes, it's her."

"Who is this?" I asked the man, pointing to Ruth.

"We were told it was a Princess of Austria, but nobody believed it. In fact, it was a bit of a scandal, a titbit my editor was happy to use in the Gazette! Do you like it? I think it's rather a poor photograph, composition wise."

"At last, some luck!" I said, to Annie. "Memorize this but without the carriage!"

"That carriage was covered in gold!" the man added. "I have never seen anything like it."

"Ready?" I asked Annie.

"Yes."

"Thank you, sir," I told the man. "If you want a good news story, I suggest you get down to the Gazette offices right now!"

With that, we left and sought a quiet street.

"Ready?" I asked Annie again.

"Let's go. I badly want to see my dad. Do you think he will be there?"

"I don't know Annie."

I held her hand, and we began to run.

***

On top of Cologne Cathedral, in 1856, John climbed inside the medieval crane. Chalcathgna spun to face him. The great beast sat between two great tread-wheels, wide enough for three men, and with his feet on a horizontal wheel.

The beast snarled at John and climbed out of the lifting apparatus.

Chalcathgna stuck forward a huge fist and smashed it straight into John's chest. John only had a moment to tense before he was sent flying back out of the crane, across the platform and crashing into a pile of blocks. He lay there, dizzy, gasping for breath and trying to find his anger, while the crane began to turn again.

Georgina staggered against the wind to come to her lover's side.

"John!"

"Pray for me or do whatever you do. Curse him if you must. I am too weak!"

Georgina trembled and put her finger tips to John's face.

"I feel some of my strength returning!" she yelled. She began to murmur something while John staggered to his feet, yelling:

"Watch out!"

The block of stone came hurtling round its arc above their heads and smashed into the pile of blocks, sending yet more onto the far side of the platform. One block fell forward, just missing John's hands and crashed through the wood at their feet.

John peered over and could see the scaffolding of the tower, stretching right down to the congregation, who now appeared to be running for cover like ants.

"Get up! Get up!" Georgina cried, taking hold of John's shoulders. At last, he felt some strength coursing through his body. He struggled to his feet and dodged the wrecking-ball block as it came round again.

The medieval crane seemed to teeter on its mounting blocks, and John saw for the first time that the crane was attached directly to the platform. The platform lifted slightly at the opposite edge to the block, each time it swung. But now, the crane mountings were tearing loose.

"This is madness!" John yelled. "He will kill himself!"

No matter how hard he tried, John could not connect with his own anger. His body stubbornly remained that of a man and only a man. He could not take on Chalcathgna directly. But as the block came round again, he saw another possibility.

He crouched on a tall block of stone, carved into a foliated finial. As the block swung past he leaped onto it and grabbed for the hook.

He missed it and fell across the top of the block as it swung. His body slithered off the block, but his desperate fingers managed to hook themselves around one of the harness ropes. With his feet hanging in space, John hung on to the block until the crane's rotation stopped for a moment. He was able to haul himself up to a kneeling position. Immediately he saw that the crane's wet rope was rotted and fraying.

"Must be the original rope," John muttered to himself. "Nearly five hundred years old! Any moment it will break, but that moment might not be soon enough!"

He could see Chalcathgna's black face sneering at him from the crane housing.

"I know what you are doing!" John yelled. "The crane is falling apart. You want to send it and everything else crashing to the ground!"

"Ha! Yes. You noticed!"

"But *you* will die too!"

"You forget, I cannot be killed in this world by human hands, and you are in no shape to take your wolf form!"

"You *will* die this time, because of this!"

From under his kudra, John drew the silver sword he had taken when Hugo had fallen and held it aloft.

"No!" Chalcathgna hissed. "It cannot be! It's impossible! That went down into the water in Hell! It was seen!"

"Yes, and I picked it up. I knew it would be useful!"

John must have been gambling, playing for time, by showing the sword. He knew it could not destroy the spirit of Chalcathgna while in serpent form, but the response of the beast must have surprised him and given him an idea. John added:

"I don't know how many have died to give you your physical body on Earth this time, but I know the Sword cannot extinguish your spirit. But I have never tried it on your current form!"

Chalcathgna's eyes narrowed.

"Even if your body survives the fall, Georgina, or I will thrust *this* straight through your heart!"

Chalcathgna howled with rage and the crane jib came to a halt with the block suspended over the edge of the Cathedral tower.

John glanced down, over 200 sickening feet below. The block swung like a pendulum, its arc extended crazily by the howling wind. Rain drove into John's face, obscuring his vision, but he saw Chalcathgna climb out through the opening and begin to climb to the roof of the crane housing. As he climbed, his weight further tilted the jib over the edge of the tower.

"John! John! No!" Georgina howled from the top of the steps. "I love you!"

The ancient crane teetered on its moorings, and the wooden platform tilted as Chalcathgna neared the top of the jib. There, he paused stood up straight and yelled some profane incantation into the storm. At first, only tiny wings sprouted from his shoulders, but as Georgina and John watched, the wings grew to an immense span, forty feet or more, and a tail extended to a great length. As they watched, Chalcathgna, the greatest Serpent, took on his blood-red serpent form and swooped upon John, who was clinging precariously to the swinging block.

"Now I am safe!" Chalcathgna hissed. "Strike me if you want. I don't care. I am not afraid of death anyway. 'Death' is just a word, and I have been around since a time when there were only a few words. I was there at the beginning. You cannot know much of life, John."

Chalcathgna's great jaw opened, and he struck out for John's head. John used a hard bind to parry with the sword held above his head. The sword clanged off the fangs of the great Serpent, almost breaking his wrist.

"We all serve the Synchronicity code John, even you! I knew, when I was young, that there was no other rhyme or purpose to life other than something already set, a perverse order that only favours the fatalists. It's tyrannical. I have fought against it, fought to be free of it, ever since. Die now and join us!"

Again, Chalcathgna lunged, and this time he jinked to avoid John's thrust and grabbed John's sword wrist.

John was on his back and stared past his attacker's eyes of fire to the rope above. It was almost frayed through, and the twisted fibres spun apart.

"The rope!" John yelled.

The Serpent ignored him and snapped his jaw shut, sending the Sword, and John's hand, spinning down into the darkness.

"Argh!" John yelled in pain. But at last, the anger he had sought, began to rise in his soul.

"No Demon! You won't win this time. No! No!"

The denial became a chant as John's body began to transform. As the blood spurted from his severed wrist, he grew into the shape of an enormous, black wolf.

The combined weight of the two bodies was too much for the old crane. A rending sound could be heard from its moorings.

Georgina, galvanised by desperation, ran to the cab and climbed inside, looking for some way to swing the jib one more time, to bring the block to safety.

But it was too late. The crane toppled over, ripping the oak planks free of the platform and came crashing down to the tower top. The jib fell below the tower edge, and the two beasts fell until the frayed rope jerked the block to a halt, swinging far below Georgina.

Chalcathgna was pinning John down, slowly forcing its jaw closer to John's heart. With his one remaining hand and legs, John fought to keep the venomous fangs from entering his flesh. The muscles in his arms bulged to a huge size as they fought against the power of the great Serpent, who now had his fangs just a few millimetres from John's fur.

Suddenly, a fistful of the rope's fibres snapped at the same time, tilting the block to one side. The Serpent slipped on the wet block, releasing its weight from John's legs for a fraction of a second. John kicked out, sending the Demon further toward the edge of the abyss. John twisted his canine body desperately and managed to get behind the neck of the beast that was pinning him down. He forced his fangs deep into the neck of the Serpent and released his own venom into its veins.

As the Serpent howled in pain and defeat, John howled in victory. He held down the serpent while the venom disabled, then weakened it and then began to shut out its dark light.

"John!" Georgina screamed, after clambering from the wrecked crane and peering over the edge. "John! It won't hold!"

John heard her voice from very far away and looked up. The last fibres spun away, and the rope broke.

The resulting jerk unsteadied John, and he staggered to keep his balance. The block began to fall into space,

but at the last moment, John leaped for the end of the
remaining crane's rope.

"John!" Georgina screamed, when his claw touched
the strands. But his claw closed on dry, rotten fibres that
refused to hold his weight. They tore away, and he fell,
into the black gloom of the stormy night.

Georgina ran, weeping, all the way down the stairs
to the plaza outside the Cathedral, but the two wrecked
bodies were lifeless, caught in death's embrace. She
cradled John's body in her arms and whispered through
her tears:

"Now I can tell you what I wanted to say."

***

Annie, and I came to a halt after jumping through
time again. We were in front of the Cathedral, more or
less where the photograph had been taken, but both of
us fell to our knees, gasping for breath.

"Never have I been so exhausted," I murmured. "I
felt something tugging at my will, and I had to focus
like never before! I just hope we got it right this time!"

"I felt something dragging us away too. It was
horrible. I thought I had lost you!"

Indeed, I had actually screamed with the pain of
concentration just before we pulled out of the
blackness, but I didn't want to admit that to Annie.

"Well, the market stalls look right," I suggested.
"And the spire is there, look. But that doesn't mean
anything yet. You know what I said about John's
premonitions of evil?"

"Of course. He used to have them when I was a kid.
It saved my life once."

"I feel terrible, sick. I feel the presence of something
very bad, malignant, evil. We have to be very, very
careful. Take my hand!"

"Did anybody see us? I don't want to be chased

again!"

"It doesn't look like it. Let's find out the date." It didn't take long to find somebody. "Excuse me! What is the date today?"

"9 April 1881 sir!"

"Thank you!" I replied

"We did it!" Annie whispered.

"Well, that's something. Now we just have to get in! That might not be easy!"

"Don't worry. There's a password, and I know it. They won't have changed it."

"Alright."

We could already see flickering light, occasionally outlining one of the Cathedral's main doors each time it opened. A black carriage with a blue shield, sporting a capital letter 'R' and five arrows in a fist, was parked next to the plaza.

"Something is going on already," I suggested.

"What time is it?"

"Nearly midnight."

"I'm guessing Ruth is already here. That's probably why you feel so sick."

"Oh. Well if things haven't progressed too far, perhaps we should try the password. Remember, I'm just your bodyguard, and I don't speak German or English. If they ask, say I am Greek."

"Alright."

"Let's go."

We were perhaps less than 100 feet from the doors when they opened, and two figures came out. They headed to our right but passed not too far away.

"Stop!" I told Annie. "Can you see?"

Both figures were dressed in kudras, but they were also wearing masquerade masks, the taller wearing a colourful, plumed mask and the shorter, a black one. I took Annie's elbow and steered her away from the

Cathedral.

"There was something I recognised about the tall one," I told her. "I don't know what … . Anyway, we have to find masks! Clearly this is being conducted like some kind of ball!"

"You certainly give a girl some challenges. I was pretty shit-hot at needlework at school though. A haberdasher, and some nifty theft should do it!"

"'Nifty?' and 'Shit-hot?' I guess it's the age-gap!"

"Never mind old man. Just find the shop!"

We were lucky to find a haberdasher within a few blocks, not so lucky that its windows were protected by a steel grate. It took me a few minutes to jimmy the lock. A few minutes later, we were sitting in a late-night café, while Annie sewed together one ornate mask and one plain one. When she finished, she announced:

"They will only hold together for a little while, I wouldn't call it so much a running stitch as a leaping one! It will have to do. Let's go!"

We reached the door of the Cathedral and had to knock.

"Yes sir?" the doorman, wearing a typical 17th Century French costume and a mask, asked.

"Nebuchadnezzar," Annie whispered.

"But you're early. I … I would have to wait for … ."

"Yes, we're early," Annie replied. "Ruth wanted it so. You better do as you're told! You know who I am?"

I was surprised by Annie's authoritative tone.

"Yes … I know who you are," the doorman replied. He looked at me suspiciously.

"He is my bodyguard. There was a change at the last moment; trouble in Jerusalem." This seemed to tilt the balance in our favour. The man nodded.

"You may pass."

The doorman looked sheepishly around him and opened the door just wide enough for us to pass. Annie nudged me and steered me to the left, toward the nave and the dirge-like tones of the organ.

"We have to hide!" Annie whispered. "I lied. Once Ruth knows I am here with an unknown man, she will be looking for us."

We found a flight of stairs to the gallery. We continued climbing to the clerestory where we hid in a niche behind a pillar. It was very uncomfortable, standing with one foot on the pillar pedestal and one, angled, to fit on the floor. After ten minutes, we had to sit down. We didn't even whisper for nearly an hour, until we heard the note of the organ change."

"It's started!" Annie whispered.

Cautiously, we crept to the carved balustrade at the edge of the clerestory and peered over.

Below us, at the transept crossing, a procession of twelve, tall, masked figures walked slowly round in a circle, each trailing a retinue of twelve shorter figures, all draped in ornate, white and gold costumes. Their crowns' rims rose to a peak, some four feet above their heads, topped by a pair of wings. One tall figure alone, wore a pure white costume.

The music from the organ changes again, and the figures processed in a line to the altar.

On the altar, a large silver cross with equal length verticals and horizontals. But as I looked, I could see it wasn't a crucifix but a star; there were shorter diagonals.

In front of the altar, lay an open, gold casket. Even with my sharp eyes, I couldn't quite make out any detail of what was inside, but it appeared to be bound in white linen.

What I could see, were some white-costumed men wearing masks, patrolling around the gallery.

"They are going to start missing you, now you are missing from the ceremony," I whispered. "We better find a better hiding-place soon.

But I could not take my eyes from the ceremony.

"You look like a wolf on the hunt," Annie whispered.

"I feel out of my depth here. Tell me a bit about what is happening here."

"They are blessing the body of the dead Angel. Later, two of the Servants will carry it to the top of the Spire and place it in a specially designed container, a spherical shape, like that on eastern orthodox Christian churches."

"Is that what they are for?"

"Only the tallest. The rest are shaped in imitation. It has always been in Ruth's plan that the tallest should serve as vessels for the resurrection of Angels. Saint Sophia in Istanbul is one of them. I don't know much more. I didn't pay much attention."

"Ruth? This was her duty? Part of the Synchronicity Code?"

"Yes. Georgina could tell you more. She is a know-it-all."

"Mm. Wait! I recognise him. It's Mara, Mara bar Serapion! Your father and I met him in Jerusalem. I thought I recognised him. Damn! I should have spoken to him at the door; told him what was happening! But he was going out. So they can leave at any time?"

"No. The doors will be locked now. Nobody will come in or go out. This is the *most sacred* of ceremonies."

"And you were trained to subvert it."

Annie didn't reply.

"Sorry, I added."

Still Annie didn't speak. I turned to her. A tear was rolling down her cheek. I put my arm round her shoulder and whispered:

"I didn't mean to say that. I'm sorry. I just feel out of my depth, and I don't know how I came to be in this situation."

"It's not that. My father. Why isn't he here? I thought he would be waiting for us. He could have at least left a sign. Do you think he survived?"

"I don't know. I wish I could say, 'Yes,' but he was not in the best condition to fight that monster. And Georgina might not have been much help. She might have turned on him at the last moment. We can only hope. Maybe he is waiting somewhere nearby. Maybe he can't help us with this or can't get into the Cathedral."

Annie nodded and added:

"It's lucky this is organised by the Council and not just Ruth. She would have changed the password if she could, but then the others would have become suspicious."

The organ's warm, reverberating chords suddenly rose to a crescendo, and all the Angels and their assistants sang at the tops of their voices. A light, so piercing that it hurt, lit up somewhere deep inside my head. I struggled to stay conscious, and after a few moments, the feeling subsided. I said:

"I wonder what the locals … ."

I bit off my own words, because the music suddenly stopped, only the echoes reverberating away to nothing in the vast choir and leaving only the sound of my voice in my ears. Annie and I looked nervously at each other.

"They're going,"

Two tall men strode forward, lifted the bound body from the casket and carried it to the same flight of steps we had ascended.

"Quick! We have to go!" I whispered.

"It's alright. There's a door, which opens onto the staircase to the Spire, at the top of the stairs. They won't come down here."

"Nevertheless, let's get back behind one of these

pillars."

After the procession had passed, almost soundlessly, climbing up to the belfry, I whispered:

"I wish we could see what they are doing up there. What happens now?"

"Not much, for twenty-four hours. The body will be placed in the container and a force-field of Angelic Will will be placed around the container which nothing can penetrate. Then they will come down."

"Will they all stay in the Cathedral? Do they *need* to?"

"I don't know if they will stay. Some might. They don't need to stay. Some will go back to their lives and times. Only Ruth and Violet Bell will definitely stay."

"Why can't we stop Violet Bell now? Kill her?"

"We could, if we can find her. You can bet Ruth has her well-hidden … ."

"Alright then, we need a hideaway for now. We'll continue this discussion later. Perhaps I will try to find her. Come on!"

Above the south transept, we found a small store room's whose door was unlocked. Moreover, it had a small leaded window, which would enable me to climb down the outside of the Cathedral if necessary. The room was faintly lit by moonlight.

"Here. Let's wedge the door shut," I told Annie, dragging some oak panels from the corner of the room to wedge under the door handle. "We'll be safe for a while. Now, tell me more about Ruth; what she and her followers believe. I need to *understand* them."

"Hm, let's see now. Well, fundamentally, they believe love is a compromise. Lust is the purest pursuit of happiness. It is the King while Secret Desire is the Queen on the chessboard of life. The chessboard is a powerful symbol and the chequered floor is used as a design throughout Satan's rituals."

"Like the floor here, in the Cathedral?"

"Yes. Evil usually has a clever way of infiltrating or subverting even the most sacred of rituals and places."

"It's strange to hear you talk like that. You sound more like a thirty-year old!"

"I'm nearer forty, intellectually!"

Annie smiled at me, and I was touched by her innocent pride. Somehow, she had hung on to her innocence for an extraordinarily long time, even in Hell, but the price was an intense isolation that seemed to shade her gaze when I stared into her eyes.

"Anyway, go on," I prompted.

"Um. There *is* a stone, a gravestone of iron, hidden in the Black Forest of Germany. I've been there. It's almost as tall as a man and has two holes for hands and one for your head. When you put your hands and head through it, they become separated spiritually from your body. Satan only needs the mind and the hands. With those, you can become completely his servant. When you put your head through the hole, you see only a beautiful white light on the other side."

"Have you tried … ."

My sentence was cut short by a banging on the door. I held Annie, and we both remained stock-still. After the door-handle had been shaken a few times, footsteps receded, and we could breathe again.

"They're searching for us," I whispered. "They'll be back."

I began to release Annie from my grasp, but she clung on, murmuring:

"Don't leave me."

I lifted her chin to look into her eyes. They implored me not to let her go.

"I have no one," she added.

"You have me," I replied.

"Oh yeah! You're a blood-sucker! I know why *you*

want me!" she joked.

We both giggled and sat down on a disused pew.

"How can you be sure I won't suck your blood?" I whispered.

"Because daddy trusted you."

She looked straight at me, and I returned her gaze. For an instant, I must have shown how pretty I thought her, because she squeezed my hand and leaned toward me. Her lips were so full and reddened by blood that I kissed her compulsively. It was almost a reflex, but she returned my kiss warmly and pulled me to her.

"Wait!" I said, pulling away. I stood up. "First of all, there's no time now and *secondly*, I'm not sure if you're even physically sixteen, and you're the daughter of my best friend!"

I must have seemed angry, because she laughed. The sound was like tinkling bells, high and sonorous.

"Sit down with me then and be quiet."

I wasn't used to being told what to do by a woman, but I sat down.

"I have to go out soon. To search for this … Violet," I murmured. "What does she look like?"

"Tall, blonde and fat! Oh, and ugly," Annie replied. Her arm had already slid round my shoulder, and she moved to sit on my lap.

"First of all," she murmured, "I know I am sixteen, because, after some training, Satan sent me to a finishing school, horrible place like a prison, somewhere in Austria for almost two years before being again taken back to 1st Century Hell. Satan wouldn't have wanted me *just* as a child! Secondly, I am a virgin. I don't want to be. And I might die tonight."

She had hit the nerve; the thought that I would probably die had occurred to me too. Fear and adrenalin carried us up into the vaults of lust or desire, who cares which?

I stood up, clasping her to me. She *was* very pretty; not as slender as Georgina, but there was more tone to her limbs and probably the rest of her body. I wondered if she had been a tomboy. I could remember what John had said about her as a child. I had always been attracted to tomboys. Her face was always animated. Her freckles added an attractive earthiness to those laughing eyes, and the whole effect was framed by those waves of brown hair.

Annie's legs were already around my waist, so I turned to lean her slight weight against the wall and unfastened my breeches. She was already pulling up her long skirt, and I saw that she wore nothing I could call underwear. I struggled to unlace her bodice, so while I kissed her neck, she took over the duty.

"But you're special, and I'm nothing, probably less than nothing!" I protested, half to myself.

"You *are* special. You just don't know it yet."

"Well, I always wanted an unattainable woman."

"I can be that."

I smiled and kissed her throat. I heard her whimper once, but she lost her virginity without protest.

"Are these a child's?" she said, releasing her breasts from her corset.

"No," I whispered.

I have to admit, I felt surprised how much adrenalin heightened my passion and how much desire took away my weariness; it had been a long time since I had made love in such a tight situation. She rose and fell on my hips like a mermaid on the bows of a ship. Her eyes rolled back until I could only see the whites through narrow slits. I remember not who climaxed first or whether we did together, but when I subsided, I was completely exhausted. I let Annie's body slide to the floor on top of mine, and there we lay. I remember murmuring:

"I have never been so tired!"

***

Those words were the last thing I remember until we woke, cold and aching.

"Wake up!" I said, shaking Annie.

We were lying together on the pew, with her dress and my overcoat covering us. She was naked, enveloped in my arms, I wearing only my breeches.

"What time is it?" she murmured dreamily.

"I don't know, but there is daylight!"

I stood up and stumbled to the window. With some difficulty, I opened the window and took in the vista of Cologne. Even without craning my neck, I could see the sky to the west was lighter.

"Sunset!" I declared. "Oh no! We've slept far too long. I knew I felt too tired. The last week has finally got to me! Anyway, we're still alive, and I presume it's still the ninth. I have to see if I can find this Violet Bell.

"But why didn't they come for us? You said they *would*."

"I don't know. But it means you're safe here. I won't be gone for more than two hours. Don't leave here!"

I pulled on my shirt, waist jacket and overcoat and climbed onto the window sill.

Annie clutched her dress to her chest and walked over to me before whispering:

"Don't be late!"

We kissed, I found a foothold below the window and lowered myself down.

With some difficulty, I grew bat claws to descend to the ground, but the stone work of the Cathedral had been so decorative that they only increased my speed, so that I soon hurried across the plaza.

I had no idea where to find Violet. My plan had been to see who was still inside and who had left the

Cathedral and try to track the absentees. It still seemed the best plan, so I hid my clothes behind a coal bunker and transformed into a large bat. It took longer than I would have liked, and then I had to find an open window, high up in the clerestory of the cathedral. But when I peered down into the aisles, I could only see Servants.

I flew over the City for over an hour, searching everywhere for the carriage with the blue shield as this seemed my best bet. But it must have been well-concealed. I returned to my clothes, empty handed and completely exhausted. I had to sit down on a rooftop to recover.

I started awake and stared at the twinkling city lights.

How long have I slept?

I had intended finding a victim to drain of blood, but now I feared I had stayed abroad too long.

Swooping past a city clock, which shoed just before 11 pm, I flew back to the store room window. The scene that met my eyes horrified me beyond words.

The room was empty, no Annie, and the door had a hole burned neatly though it, which was big enough to admit a large person.

Annie! Oh shit! Oh no! What an Idiot I have been!

After I had cursed myself for a full minute, I forced my breathing to an even rhythm and tried to think.

Where would they take her? Perhaps to the ground floor somewhere?

I crept to the charred door and stuck my head cautiously through the hole. Looking left and right, I could see nobody close by, so I continued on to the balustrade and peered into the nave below.

Many more people now, including some of the taller ones; Angels I presume.

I suddenly felt incredibly alone. I have to make

assumptions and guesses, now that Annie wasn't with me.

I hesitated.

I could transform to a bat again and fly down, or I could cast the cloak, but I am too tired, and the Angels would easily spot me. Wait! Maybe the tower?

I turned left and crept toward the eastern end of the cathedral. I was not far from the tower when I saw him. A man, wearing a mask, was standing guard over a small, oak door. On the door, somebody had roughly painted a star, like that on the altar.

I was just wondering how to get past him when a commotion broke out below. One of the tall figures, walking remarkably similarly to Ruth, was striding across the nave, closely followed by three servants. She was berating them about something, turning to them and wagging her finger. Her voice boomed around the Cathedral, but I couldn't be sure it was Ruth, so many echoes were there. I backed away from the man in case he heard too and came to investigate.

When the voice had gone, I crept toward him again. I took a silver coin from my waist jacket, cast the cloak and tossed the coin at the guard's feet.

Quickly pressing myself into the niche behind a fluted column decoration, I waited like a shadow for him to pass. He didn't even glance up.

I tip-toed past him, ran past the door and on to an arch at the end of the clerestory. Through the arch, I found a stairwell. Half-expecting these to take me up to the spire, I was disappointed that they only led down.

I turned to retrace my steps. The guard was still there. But then I noticed something blue, on the stone floor, a few feet in front of me. Still casting the cloak, I stooped and picked it up; a small patch of blue cloth with three holes in it.

Annie's dress! And three holes, one large and two,

small. That story about the gravestone. Nobody else could possibly know she told me that. Unless Ruth can hear everything!

I inspected the cloth more closely. The holes were torn, not cut, and too crudely torn to be sure. My initial excitement and hope was followed by disappointment. I couldn't be sure.

I have to think carefully. If it is a clue, then Annie must have left it here for a purpose. Why? The door. Maybe she went through it.

Whether being escorted, or on her own, I had to assume Annie had gone through the oak door.

But then I heard the ominous sound of more footsteps. A second guard was approaching the first. With no time to waste, I crept up behind the first guard and threw another coin behind the one approaching. They both spun to face the strange sound, and I tried the door, praying it wasn't locked. I was in luck.

I closed the door silently and sped along a short tunnel to a second door, which opened onto a landing. To my relief, there were stairs, leading up.

I have wasted too much precious time! Up!

I took the steps, three at a time, until I tired and was reduced to one. I don't know how many steps it was, but after very many, I reached the belfry.

There, I was rewarded with another small square of blue cloth, tucked into the crevice between some decorated skirting on the wall and the floor.

Annie! I'm coming!

On and on, up the endless stairs I climbed. Several times, I heard voices below me. I walked faster, and the sound receded. I wanted to take the form of a dog, but I didn't know what I would have to deal with. It seemed that everything was drawing to one stupendous climax, the moment when either Good or Evil would triumph. Incredibly, for the first time in my life, I knew that I was firmly on the side of Good.

When I thought I would have to stop to recover my breath, I finally reached an open space with balconies, not far below the base of the spire. I staggered out onto the balcony and peered over the edge.

Cologne twinkled like a fairy city below me. From somewhere, a wind had whipped up and tossed my hair across my face. I looked above me and below for any sign of Annie. Not far below me, a faint yellow light flickered briefly from one of the stairwell windows. My pursuers would be here at any moment. I ran right round the balcony but saw no sign of Annie.

Stumbling back inside the tower, I saw several flights of iron stairs leading up to two long, wooden ladders. These led to a vaulted ceiling, so far above that I had to crane my neck to make it out in the gloom.

My stomach felt sick at the idea of climbing the so many more precarious rungs in my state, but I had *no* choice. I had to go further up!

That there *could be* somewhere *further up* seemed quite improbable and almost made me laugh. I wondered if I were close to hysteria.

"Damnation John!" I swore as I grabbed the handrail of the first step. "You *would* have to get me into this mess. I hope it's all worth it!"

I stepped up to the first ladder and then took hold of its rungs as if it were a lover. If I craned my neck now, I could just make out where the wooden contraption disappeared through a ring in the centre of the vault. I almost fell over backwards, so dizzy was I. I swore with each step I took, swaying from side to side. I found myself trembling when I climbed through the ring, just as a lantern suddenly lit up the vaulted room below me.

"Hey! You! Stop!" somebody shouted.

I stepped backward and ran to another balcony. I ran right round the tower, looking for Annie; up and down.

But I couldn't see her.

"Annie! Annie! I yelled at the top of my voice. The wind seemed to take it and turn it into something that sounded unfamiliar.

Running back inside, I peered up into the gloom. Only by the faint light of stars and a pale blue glow far, far above me, could I make out the lattice-work of the hollow spire. It was beautiful, but I had no time to admire the brilliance of its designers or builders.

I could possibly have climbed the latticework, but I knew there had to be yet another ladder. I ran back outside to look for it. I walked round the balcony again, which was half-enclosed by waste-high iron fence-work. If I felt sick before, now waves of nausea crashed over me. I had to go up despite my exhaustion and the extreme height. I hung on to rail, so as not to fall from dizziness and edged round the balcony, but I had to look down to check my feet didn't snag anything.

I saw it before I knew I was looking at it; another tiny piece of blue cloth. This one had no holes in it, but I was in no doubt it was Annie's. It was not at the base of the ladder, and I concluded that she might have climbed over the fence.

"Hey! Vampire! You shouldn't be up here! You can't escape!" a voice hollered inside the tower, only feet from me.

I scrambled over the fence and down to a decoration of foliage that I would later learn was called a crocket. The tower was covered in them, breaking up its stony lines and offering a foothold to a bird, bat or scrambling, desperate person.

Extending the claws of a bat with my last reserves of energy, I climbed down a narrow gable over a high arch. This brought me to a square stone column, perhaps four feet in width. I had considerable difficulty traversing this before climbing over the lip of another arch to a secondary spire, which only rose to perhaps fifty feet above me.

"Annie! Annie!" I yelled again, desperate.

She can't be out here anyway! She must have fallen!

I had been about to turn round when I thought I heard a sound, more like a bird than a human. But I had to be sure. I climbed out onto the secondary spire, which was much more highly decorated than even the main tower. It was heavily fluted, like a set of organ pipes, and on the extreme outside, was another gable end, extending up some ten feet. Behind this, I saw something shimmer in the moonlight. I climbed toward it. I can climb almost anything with bats talons, but I could no longer raise the energy for any kind of talons and was wrenched from the stonework by a sudden gust of wind. I slid down a leaded gulley and only caught the edge of a decoration a moment before going over the edge. I had to stop for a moment to steady my nerves before stepping into the crevice and reaching out for the blue cloth.

"Annie!" I yelled, trembling.

***

Annie clutched me tightly. I could feel her shaking uncontrollably as well, from the cold.

"You're trembling too! Are you cold?" she asked me.

"No. Weak. That was very clever and brave of you; the blue cloth," I said into her ear over the howling wind.

"I thought you wouldn't come. I couldn't think what else to do!"

"We're not safe!" I yelled. "Come on. Better to face them than a fall to sure death!"

I felt her laugh, and she replied:

"You think so? How long?"

"How long until they destroy the body?"

"Yes!"

"*Minutes*! "They're up there now. I'm going up!"

"They must have waited until you went," Annie suddenly blurted. "Ruth came for me, but I climbed out of the window and down to the floor below. That was when I had the idea about the grave stone."

"Yes. Good idea. It's interesting that Ruth waited for me to be gone."

"Yes. Maybe she fears you. It could be, because you are not too unlike John, something she doesn't understand or have control over."

"Maybe. Take my hand!"

It was a heart-stopping struggle to get back to the platform. Several times, Annie ended up dangling from my finger-tips.

"I don't know how you even managed to get here!" I yelled.

She indicated I should be silent, with her index finger on her lips.

"Look!" she said, pointing. I looked in the direction of her finger and saw a slight, blonde woman, in a violet dress, climbing one of two towers which went all the way to the topmost finial of the Cathedral.

"It's Violet! We're too late!"

"No we're not! Come on."

We only had the lip of the arch to climb and then to scale a short section of decoration to the fence. But I could see now that six burly men, wearing masks and wielding various weapons, including pistols, were facing out over the fence, watching for us. One of them spotted us and aimed his pistol.

"Duck!" I yelled.

The bullet chipped a sliver of stone off the tower which grazed my cheek. I glance up and saw Ruth's face, peering from the balcony next to the gunman.

"Will our luck never *change*?" I asked myself.

"*Nothing* is going our way! I despair!"

Again, I felt as if I were falling into an abyss from which I could never escape. But Annie must have heard me somehow, because she squeezed my elbow.

Now, think rationally. At least the wind is in our favour. That's probably the only reason he missed. I have to have blood, or I can't do this.

With every few seconds we delayed, Violet Bell climbed one step closer to the pinnacle and the body of the dead Angel!

I thought for a moment and told Annie:

"There's only one way we can do this," I yelled. "I am going to create a diversion, and then you have to get up that spire. I won't be able to help you, because I will have to fight Ruth, *if* I can first kill *all* her henchmen. It's a tall order … ."

Annie clutched at me but nodded slowly.

"But there is something I need first."

"What?"

"Blood. Yours. Will you let me?"

"How much. Will it kill me?"

"No. Just a few pints. As little as I can."

"What do you want *me* to do?" she shouted into my ear.

"I'll do it.

Lifting up the hem of her dress, I sank my fangs into her thigh just above her femoral artery. I felt her shudder as I swallowed the first mouthful of her blood, and when I looked up, she gripped the stonework behind her with gritted teeth.

"God! Do all women feel like this?" she gasped.

I felt my strength returning with each draft of the precious liquid of life but something more; I felt a cleanness, a power that I had never experienced. I looked up in wonder at Annie when I had finished and yelled:

"Darling, you are special. I feel that I have been reborn!"

I gently replaced the hem of her dress and wiped my mouth before kissing her.

"I hope you enjoyed yourself!" she replied, giggling.

We edged around the decoration and I pointed to the spire, telling Annie:

"Wait here until you see a clear path to the ladder, inside the spire. Don't look back! Whatever happens, keep going!"

"Alright. Zosimyache?"

"I love you."

"That was what I was going to say!"

"Say it then."

"I love you."

I kissed her once, hard, and began to traverse, out of the enemy's sight, round to the opposite side of the tower. I didn't want to think how hard it was going to be for Annie to climb to the very top of the spire. I was already over 300 feet above the City. I glanced up to the very top of the spire. It had to be another two hundred feet, at least.

At least my shape-shifting can be used for something good! Even if Ruth is the end of me! Come to think of it, who the hell is Ruth!

I didn't have time to think about this. I peered around a stone ornament, and I saw a gunman's barrel, pointing directly at me. I yanked my head back just in time to hear the bullet whizz past my ear and ricochet off something below me.

Now is as good a time as any!

Balancing on a gable peak, I stripped off my clothes. The wind made the air icy cold. I stuffed them, haphazardly, into a crevice and focused on the shape of a bear.

For a frightening effect, I decided a deep booming

growl was in order. Then I clambered around the ornament and leaped for the base of the platform. With all my strength, I hoisted my bear-body over the fence and smashed into the face of the gunman who had seen me. He had been too terrified to let off more than one poorly-aimed shot, which passed straight through my ear. I snapped his neck with one swipe.

"There he is!" Ruth yelled, now wearing a red dress. "In the shape of bear! Don't be afraid. Kill him!"

She must have been looking round the corner, and I wanted to get to her, but I had five men left to kill.

"Some of you, round the back!" Ruth hollered over the roar of the wind.

It was the break I needed. It gave me a few more precious moments with the three men in front of me. I barrelled into them, taking only one bullet wound to my neck. Fortunately, it had missed any main arteries.

All three men lay beneath me, arms and legs flailing. One or two bullets were fired, but one man fell, limp, immediately. He had been hit. I gored a second, but the man at the back managed to slip loose and backed to the corner, just in front of Ruth's venomous face.

I took a swipe at the gunman, just as his pistol-chamber clicked over.

I saw the bullet exit the barrel and even the puff of smoke from the rear of the chamber.

They say time almost stops when you are about to die, and I felt strangely ready for death. The bullet almost seemed like a friend as it sped towards my head.

But then I heard a voice inside me. It said:
"Move!"

I yanked my head to the side, twisting at the same time. The bullet grazed my face, shearing through my flesh like a knife through butter. It must have been deflected by my skull, because my head was jerked to the side, burning the muscles in my neck with the whiplash. My head smashed into the ironwork on the inside of the platform, and my vision went black. But I was alive. The voice had been female.

I struggled to grip something, blind as I was, and my paws closed around something smooth and hard. I began clumsily to climb. Before I had been shot, I had noticed the edifice of the spire consisted of a hollow quatrefoil stonework design.

Another bullet ripped into my back, making me howl with pain. Blindly, I climbed on. I shook my head and my vision cleared slightly. The nearest four-leafed clover shaped quatrefoil opening was a few feet above me. As my claws gripped the inside edge of the quatrefoil, another bullet ripped into the stonework from my right, showering my face with grit.

With one more push, I managed to get my head and forepaws through the hole. Bullets were striking the stonework all round me. I had to shrink my size slightly to get all the way through, and then I was dropping to the stone floor.

Blood was pouring down my cheek and from my back, into my fur, but I could still move, and while I could, I wasn't going to abandon Annie.

I prowled round the inside of the tower and arrived at the arch which led onto the balcony. I wondered, briefly, if the enemy still had the stomach for a fight.

I knew the answer when a man leaped into the opening, wielding both a gun and a sword.

"Agh!" he yelled, before firing two shots. One shot missed me, the other ripped into my belly.

This is getting too much!

He pulled the trigger again, but instead of the report of a shot, there was only a 'click.' He threw down the pistol and lunged at me with the sword.

In all honesty, I don't think he expected to fight a bear who was also an expert swordsman. I might not have had his dexterity, but a bear can move fast when its will is set. I carefully performed a soft bind on his second strike and then slid my wrist along the blade to grab the hilt. His hand was crushed before he released his grip, but I was already bringing my paw up in a smashing blow to his head. His neck snapped, and his head fell backward, followed by his limp body; I had no time for niceties.

The last two men were still outside. I stuck my head outside and glanced up at the ladder. I could see that in fact, there were two ladders, a long way to the right of the archway. Annie hands and face were dim shapes, less than fifty feet beneath the spherical container at the top of the Spire. She still needed time.

I roared in the archway and rumbled round the balcony for one last attack.

The last two men, shielding Ruth, both held only swords.

She must be scared. She is using them, letting them fight to the last man.

"Hold him!" she shouted. Her black hair was being whipping around her face by gusts of the ice-cold wind. Her green eyes narrowed, and she turned her back to them.

I charged. Both men aimed strikes at my legs. One changed direction at the last moment and thrust toward my heart.

Not an expert but the better of the two. I will take him first.

I executed an extremely clumsy but effective hard bind and flung his blade tip out, over the fence. He screamed in agony and let the sword fall. His wrist was broken.

The second blade cut into my thigh, but it was a feeble strike, drawing no more than a trickle of blood.

With what felt like my last burst of energy, I crushed

the skull of the first man in my jaws and stove in the ribs of the other, who was now prone underneath me.

***

I felt weary beyond measure. I felt more like sleeping than at any other time in my life, but I knew I couldn't. I shambled round to the two ladders, which were constructed of metal, and stared up to the Ruth's vanishing shape.

With a deep sigh, I put one paw on the first rung and took my first step up.

Immediately, the wooden rungs protested at my weight. I felt brackets tearing at the bolts that held them to the stone. At this height, that was the most alarming feeling! I briefly wondered if a vampire could die while falling from a great height, but I forced myself on.

The wind wailed round me, obscuring all but its own banshee sound. That was why I didn't hear the feet beneath me. Something grabbed at my foot. I turned and saw the man who I thought had been shot by one of his companions. Clearly, he had only been stunned. His hair was smeared with blood, but he fought like a demon. I kicked his hand, but still he hung on.

Suddenly, a section of the ladder, not built to carry the weight of a bear, broke away from its rusted mooring above me. It leaned out, almost tipping me off. There was the sound or rending metal. I had no more time.

I backed down the slightly and grabbed the man by the arm. I yanked him to one side of the ladder, and he let go whereupon I simply let him fall. He didn't make a sound as he vanished into darkness.

By now, I had lost the will and energy to remain in bear form. It was probably just as well, because, as I turned to climb again, the ladder bent away from the Spire even more. I was barely able to grab the end of the section above before the bent section of ladder fell away into space below me. Hanging by one human hand, I felt, for a moment, as if I would like to fall; it would be easier than climbing. But then a will, not my own, kicked me into motion, and I swung my legs until I could wrap them around the second ladder. Supporting my weight like this for a few moments was enough to allow me to grab hold of a rung with the other hand, and I stayed in that position, gasping for breath.

Three bullet wounds, freezing to death and tired beyond measure! Is it worth attempting to catch Ruth?

But I climbed on.

When I craned my neck, I could see flashes of red and white light, 100 feet above me. I could no longer see Annie, so I knew she must already be fighting Violet.

I was closing on Ruth, perhaps 30 feet above me.

"Ruth! Stop!" I yelled. "I don't know your part in this is, but you can't let Satan get the upper hand. Ruth!"

"Ha!" she shouted down. "You really know nothing, do you?"

"About the Synchronicity Code? I know … it is your part to build things, not … destroy them!"

I was trying to slow her down, but she was almost at the container. I made the mistake of looking down. For a moment, a dizziness completely overwhelmed me. The perspectives were so strange that I couldn't tell anymore which was up and which way down. I felt as if I were about to float away from the Spire. I also felt the slight contents of my stomach start to drift up my throat.

"Oh God!" I muttered. It was the first time I had ever said that. I put my forehead to the rung for a moment before climbing on.

I was gaining on Ruth, and it was clear I had to stop

her. I didn't know who or what she was. Could she be an Angel, or was she some kind of Servant? The latter seemed unlikely, given the power she demonstrated in Hell. There, if anything, she seemed to have as much power as *any* Angel. But here, she seemed strangely powerless. Perhaps, because here they were almost human, the only twelve *real* people on Earth!

I checked myself over, as is a warrior's custom, while I climbed. My head was only grazed, a bullet had gone through my chest, just beneath my ribs, and passed out the other side, but I couldn't tell what had happened to my back. I was still climbing, and that was a blessing.

Now I was less than ten feet behind Ruth, but she was negotiating some kind of platform before the final climb of about 50 feet.

I reached the platform and scaled round to a single metal ladder, which led to the pinnacle,

Ruth was just a few feet ahead of me, the hem of her red dress billowing out in the wind. A particularly strong gust almost pulled her from the ladder, and she swung precariously from the side.

I leaped up and grabbed her foot. It was icy cold, but I felt as if my hand had been burned. I let go.

Ruth straightened herself to climb again and I prepared to grab her again, but my attention was distracted by the sight of Annie's head appearing over a set of crockets, just below the spherical container.

"Annie!" I yelled, but my word was whipped away by the wind.

Ruth was now putting on a spurt to reach the platform, so I raced to catch her fist. My hand was inches from her ankle when she hauled herself on to the metal surface, spun round and kicked at my face.

I ducked, narrowly avoiding losing some teeth. I peered up at Ruth and saw that she was muttering some incantation.

I knew this meant trouble. I thought now would be a good time to transform into a bat, so I forced myself to focus, but I wasn't able to effect any change in my physiology at all. I stared hard at my fingers, and they remained just fingers, not talons. It could have been my weariness, but I felt that something was blocking my thoughts.

I lunged for top rung of the ladder, and my hand slipped off! It was as if the metal rungs were coated in grease. I tried again. If I had not been able to encircle it completely with my fingers, I would not have been able to grip it at all.

Ruth spun round and ran to the last stretch of metal rungs, whereupon she began to climb again.

"I'm coming Anni-… !" My words were cut off when I slipped again.

At last I reached the platform, but walking along it was like skating on ice. Ruth's magic was working against me. By the time I started on the first rung, she was passing through a gap between the double-row of crockets. I could no longer see Annie, but I thought I heard a scream above me.

At first, I had just as much trouble gripping the last set of rungs, but slowly they became less slippery. Again, I thought I heard that female voice in my head, whispering incantations. Was somebody helping *me* at last? It felt that way as my climbing speeded up. I was gaining on Ruth's ankles again.

She's no climber! I can do this!

I climbed through the gap between the lower set of crockets and lunged for Ruth's ankles again. This time, I caught her and dragged her to a sitting position on a small platform, beneath where the ladder sidestepped the upper crockets.

I am not innately violent, and I hate killing women,

so I tried tact:

"That's as far as you go Ruth!"

"Ha! You'll have to kill me *vampire*!"

"And that won't be easy, I'm guessing. But I'll do it I have to!"

From the corner of my eye, I saw the force field, encircling the Spire pinnacle. Its surface shimmered slightly in the moonlight, as if it were formed by writhing waves of electrical charge. I could see now that the white glow was from Annie and the red from Violet, both within the field. I could also see that the hatch to the container was open, and that Violet, blonde hair like a halo in the field's charge, was half inside, hung on to by a determined but half naked Annie.

I vaguely wondered how on Earth they had both managed to climb so high, but then I remembered that they were bred for a special purpose, perhaps for this single moment.

"Neither of us can enter the field," Ruth yelled.

"How do you know? Have you tried?"

"I know at least that I cannot! Don't you understand anything?"

She's trying to delay me.

"John didn't understand either. You're both pawns in a game you do not understand! But John died without even knowing what he was fighting *for*!"

Her words cut me like a knife.

"Dead? John? You *know* this?

"Yes. I have seen his body."

I looked into her emerald eyes. I felt revulsion for my own sudden desire for her. But through this desire, I saw that she told the truth. Or at least I believed it so. I felt a terrible despair creeping round my heart like a black fist. It was difficult to breath and harder to speak:

"And what are you fighting for? Simply to allow Violet, one of Satan's creations, to stop an Angel being resurrected, *as* was written in the Synchronicity Code? Are you Satan?"

The thought had occurred to me several times.

"No!" She laughed, and it rippled away into the night, louder than the wind.

This woman is more terrible and beautiful than any I could have ever imagined. My love for Annie is false. I can only love Ruth. Ruth is all, and I am nothing if not a simple slave to serve her every desire.

But I shook myself. The words in my head were false and yelled:

"Annie! I'm here! I will try to enter the field!"

"Hurry. She's too strong for me!"

"Hold on. Just a few more minutes now. Annie, if we make it, we still might die. I love you, always!"

There was no answer, so I looked for a way past Ruth. There was no doubt she had some powers, but I was prepared to risk anything. I lunged at her but she held out her hand, and I was thrown back as if hit in the gut by a charging elephant. I slammed into the rail at the end of the platform and hunched over, winded for a while.

"Are you, then, Ruth, the Angel?" I finally gasped.

"Ah. Bright boy! Brighter than John!"

"No. We both suspected it but we expected more from an Angel!"

"Hm. Witty as well as clever. Maybe I should have taken more interest in *you* in Jerusalem! Hurry Violet! There are only minutes left!"

It was my turn to smile.

"Yes, why were you so interested in John? I never understood why you seduced him."

"Ha! I didn't have to. I was curious about him. I wasn't sure yet what to do with him, so I imprisoned him. Now, I think I must be going!"

She turned and put one foot on the last ladder.

I sought something I could use against her, a loose railing perhaps, but there was nothing. And I was naked. I focused on becoming a bear. It wasn't possible, but I felt that a wolf was, and within seconds I was jumping for her heels.

Bad luck! Wolves can't climb!

But with my second jump, my jaw closed round her ankle. I let my venom enter her veins, but my teeth became icy cold, as if the liquid were instantly frozen. Then, a foul-tasting liquid began to seep into *my* mouth! I held on and dragged her back to the platform. She screamed with frustration. Her red dress caught on a bolt and tore. She turned to me:

"Zosimyache, remember the Minotaur's cave at Skotino in Greece. Remember how you were curious enough to explore it by torchlight well before the time of Christ?"

"I remember," I growled.

"You should have kept going. All the other vampires did, and they found their way to join the others in the Underworld. That is your natural home. Only you were foolish enough to stay above ground, to think that you were not evil. Now you are lost! You think you can be blessed? God nor Jesus will bless you! You are not part of the Synchronicity Code, and you never were!"

I shook my head, not wanting to hear her. Her words struck too close to the truth.

"You were a mistake!" she spat and turned away.

"No! No! No!" I told myself.

"She's lying!" the little voice inside me said.

I took a deep breath and put my foot on the rung after her, letting myself resume the shape of a naked man.

Suddenly, a blinding white vertical beam of light pierced the sky from the tip of the Spire. Several things happened at the same time; the force field expanded and changed colour to a ghostly white, Ruth uttered something I didn't understand in a foul language, and she began to grow taller.

Ruth stepped out onto one of the upper foliate projections and howled an incantation from the depths of her soul. She continued to expand, and her red dress became a white mantle of the purest white, decorated with gold. Upon her head was a crown of white-gold, and from her back sprung long white wings.

I was aware that the air around me was crackling with energy and that the field boundary was fast approaching me. Below the city was thrown into stark black and white relief by the burning white beam of light, as if the vista, from horizon to horizon, were blanched from shock.

***

My senses were overwhelmed. Ruth was hunched as if to leap and then I could see why. The field boundary had almost reached her.

With a cry of anguish, she leaped from the edge and rose upon a downward draft of wind from her vast wings. Even as I watched, they grew in length until they were 100 feet across or more.

She is an Angel!

She pointed her long finger at me, and a bolt of light hit me in the chest. The pain was beyond measure, and I was slammed back against the Spire. Again, she fired, and I nearly passed out. One more hit, and I would be gone. I said a quick prayer and lifted my eyes to Heaven.

"Zosimyache! Hang on!"

I though the pretty voice was Annie, but I couldn't see how she could help me. I heard the voice again. It was coming from below.

Ruth hovered in front of me like a vision from the

Bible. She was truly an awesome sight.

"God is truly wondrous!" I heard myself saying.

A thin beam of white light sliced through the air from below me and hit Ruth square in her heart.

At the same time, the beam boundary passed over me, and I was blinded for a moment.

When I could see again, Ruth was far away from the Spire. The field boundary approached her, but its strength appeared to be fading. I prayed it would be strong enough to kill her.

"Zosimyache! It's me!"

The source of the voice appeared on the platform and helped me to my feet. It was Georgina! She looked perhaps 40 years old but she was still beautiful.

"It was you that helped me!" I muttered.

"Come on. We have to help Annie!"

I climbed, and Georgina followed me.

I heard Ruth screaming some profanity and I looked round. Though still a blinding white vision, her heard was completely black. As I looked, the blackness spread out to her body.

I hauled myself desperately up the last few rungs and reached the container entrance. Annie was on top of Violet, whose hands were inside the beam of light. She was attempting to rip a cloth covering from the large body, curled in the foetal position within.

The light in the container was a chaos of white and red light, and I could taste the energy on my tongue.

I tried to grab Annie, to pull her back, but I was thrown away by an explosion of pure energy.

"I can help!" Georgina screamed.

I hardly remember what came next. I remember Georgina scrambling past me, and I tried to help her, but then I saw Ruth approaching us. She was still airborne, but as the blackness spread to her wings, she seemed to struggle for height. With the spread of blackness her form became more grotesque, demonic.

"No! No! No!" she screamed, as she struggled to reach us.

I thought she would fall into the abyss, but at the last moment, she reached for, and grabbed, the very end of the crocket.

There was nothing left that I could do except sink my teeth into her once more and release all my dream of death.

As she clambered onto the stonework, I took on the form of a wolf once more, helped by Georgina's energy, and sank my teeth into Ruth's arm.

"This dream is for you!" I growled as the poison slipped easily into her veins.

"No! No! No!" she screamed.

From her nails, claws extended, and she raked my flesh with them. I felt a poison enter my flesh, but it was less potent than mine. The two poisons fought each other.

"Annie!" I growled. Even though I knew Annie couldn't hear me, somehow, I hoped I could lend my will to hers.

From the corner of my eye I could see Georgina's fingers on Annie's thigh. While Georgina murmured in complete concentration, Annie held Violet's hands back from the body. Both their arms were shaking with the effort of struggle.

Violet was underneath Annie and brought her head up under Annie's chin.

"A move worthy of any professional wrestler!" I noted. Time seemed to slow almost to a stop; everything was in slow motion.

To my horror, I saw that my paws were becoming hands; I was losing my will to be in animal form. I bit harder and released the last of my poison before my teeth became human canines, and I let go my grip on

Ruth. She still clung to the platform edge, but her strength was fading. My poison had proved the stronger. Again, she was merely a woman in a red dress, flailing around with her legs for a purchase they would never find. Suspended more than 500 feet above the ground, she must have wondered what was going to happen to her when she fell.

I took my eyes from her and saw that the vertical beam of light was suddenly widening and, if anything, intensifying. Everything was bathed in the most piercing, blinding white light. It seemed to burn the nerves in the back of my skull.

"Just a few more seconds!" I screamed.

Georgina's incantation lifted above the howl of the wind, and then the white beam stopped. The body was gone, and Violet collapsed to the floor of the container, her fists clenched in frustration and despair. Ruth was hanging by one hand, but her grip on the platform finally gave out, and she fell. I turned to Annie, who was weeping, folded upon herself in a kneeling position. She was clutching her arm, so I wanted to reach her, but Georgina pushed me out of the way, lunging for the edge of the platform

"She's gone!" I yelled.

I glanced over the side and saw Ruth, falling into the dark night, her arms and legs flailing.

"She can't die!" Georgina wailed.

I didn't know if she meant that Ruth wasn't able to die or that Georgina wouldn't let her.

Georgina muttered something and pointed her index finger toward the falling Angel.

To my astonishment, I saw the Angel's vertical path deflected, and Ruth smashed into the side of the hollow stonework, bounced a few times and then seem to catch on some obstacle.

"That would have killed her!" I said.

I turned back to the two girls in the container. I gently clutched Annie's arms, and she screamed in agony. A released my grip, and she fell back, into my arms.

"It's broken," she said, holding her left arm.

"Brave girl. You won! *We* won! It's all over!"

"She told me my daddy's dead! Is it true?"

"I don't know Annie."

"It's true!" Georgina shouted. "I was there!"

Of course.

"You're bleeding!" Annie said into my ear.

"He'll live!" Georgina said.

Annie and I both looked at each other, astonished that Georgina heard us, but then John did say she was a Sorceress.

A movement from the corner of my eye caught my attention.

Violet was up and ran round to the other side of the container. She leaped down to the platform, a jump of perhaps twenty feet.

As she jumped, I caught a brief glimpse of a pretty face with beautiful, but cruel, eyes. Her blonde hair flew out behind her violet dress like a mane as she fell. She landed in a heap but picked herself up and began to climb down.

* * *

Annie and I clutched each other, exhausted. The wind began to drop, and soon it was no more than a whisper. With the subsidence of adrenalin, I began to shake uncontrollably from the cold.

"What now?" Annie whispered.

"We must go down," I replied though chattering teeth.

"I'll help you both," Georgina said.

I had forgotten her. I turned to her and said:

"Thank you Georgina. I never expected your help."

"You mean you never expected me to help! Ha! To be honest, I nearly didn't come. I have a good life now; married with a lovely daughter who is nearly fifteen! I had been preparing for this moment for twenty years, after John died. I felt I owed it to him, but when the time came, it was difficult to leave!"

We started down, Georgina leading. The City twinkled so invitingly below. We were not far from the base of the Spire.

"Jesus! That was close!" I told Annie.

"That's the first time I have heard you sound religious!"

"I met Jesus once. I will tell you about it later!"

"Hey!" yelled a voice from the balcony below.

I looked down. I recognised the face.

"Mara bar Serapion!" I yelled back.

We reached him, but he faced Georgina first, saying:

"You did well. Very well."

I looked daggers at Georgina and interjected:

"I really don't understand! Why the *hell* did you save *Ruth*?"

Georgina didn't answer.

"We can't let *another* Angel die!" Mara replied.

At last, my feet were firmly on the stone floor, and I collapsed. I felt I could go no further.

"I will send a doctor up for you!" Mara announced. "That was very well done Zosimyache!"

"So was that what was planned in the Synchronicity Code?" I asked as he disappeared down the ladder.

"The Code only plans for eventualities, it doesn't predict them! Good bye for now!"

"I still don't understand you!" I said, turning to Georgina. She was busy putting her jumper on Annie, whose bodice had been ripped down to her waist by Violet.

"Hey! How about me!" I said. "I'm completely naked!"

"You're a man!"

The term 'man' sounded comfortable to me for the first time in my life. I smiled.

"What will you do now?" I asked Georgina.

"Oh. I am finished with magic. I just want a quiet life. The CPV bothered me when I got back, last time, but eventually they lost interest. I will go back to my family. I have to wait a few years here for a Gate, but I quite like it here. Last time I found a nice German man. He, at least, will be pleased to see me!" Georgina smirked and moved to tend my wounds.

"But I thought you were married?" Annie interjected.

"Girl, you have a lot to learn!" Georgina replied. I smirked.

"Oh, I nearly forgot," Georgina said, pulling something out of her coat pocket. "John's little black book!!"

"He's dead?" Annie asked.

"Yes. Sorry Annie."

For the first time, I detected some melting of the icy distance between the two women.

"Somehow, I knew it," Annie replied.

I watched for tears, but I think she was saving them for a private moment. A smile that passed across her features was pure bravado. I hugged her tighter for it.

"Can you tell me about his death," Annie asked.

After Georgina had retold the story of John's last fight on the Cathedral tower, I began to read John's book.

"And how about you two?" Georgina suddenly asked.

"I need food, blood, something to drink and a warm bed," I replied.

"Me too, except the blood," Annie added. "Then, Zosimyache has to fulfil his duty, and take me back to Nevers. I'm not sure after that. I have to find out more about these powers I am supposed to have. I'm not sure yet where I fit in!"

"Your nephew, Michael, will need help, without John. Perhaps this will be a new dawn for Ordo Lupus. What next for you *two*?" Georgina asked. Annie looked at me.

"I have some unfinished business in 2022," I replied. "Then, I fancy a visit to my old home in what is now called *ancient Greece*! But I think I might drop in on Annie first."

"I think a few weeks holiday in Never would be good for you," Annie added. "It's very beautiful in the summer."

I smiled, took Annie's hand and kissed it.

"But I still don't understand who Ruth was," I said. "I mean, I know now she is an Angel, but why was she trying to stop some poor innocent Angel from being resurrected?"

"You still don't understand, do you?" Georgina replied. "I didn't want to tell you at first, because I didn't want John to question my motives. When he was dead, and my mind was finally set, I didn't want you to know what you were dealing with in case you got cold feet. I would imagine Annie's reasons were the same for not telling you who the dead Angel is."

"No," Annie interjected. "I never quite got round to it."

"The dead Angel," Georgina whispered, "was planning to kill Ruth. But she got there first. The dead Angel was Satan!"

***

Appendix

1 Mara bar 'Serapion

Mara bar 'Serapion, (Classical Syriac: ܡܪܐ ܒܪ ܣܪܦܝܘܢ), sometimes spelled Mara bar Sarapion, was an Assyrian Stoic philosopher in the Roman province of Syria. He is only known from a letter he wrote in Syriac to his son, who was also named Serapion, which allegedly refers to Jesus Christ (possibly the only eye-witness account of Jesus Christ).

Find links for Mara bar 'Serapion here:
http://bit.ly/or3cont#mara

2 Place de la Révolution

The Place de la Concorde (French pronunciation: [plas də la kɔ̃kɔʁd]) is one of the major public squares in Paris.

During the French Revolution the statue of Louis XV of France was torn down and the area renamed Place de la Révolution. The new revolutionary government erected the guillotine in the square, and it was here that King Louis XVI was executed on 21 January 1793.

Find links for Place de la Révolution here:
http://bit.ly/or3cont#placede

3 Knights Templar

The Poor Fellow-Soldiers of Christ and of the Temple of Solomon (Latin: Pauperes commilitones Christi Templique Salomonici), commonly known as the Knights Templar, the Order of Solomon's Temple (French: Ordre du Temple or Templiers) or simply as Templars, were among the most wealthy and powerful of the Western Christian military orders and were prominent actors in Christian finance. The organization existed for nearly two centuries during the Middle Ages.

Officially endorsed by the Roman Catholic Church around 1129, the Order became a favoured charity throughout Christendom and grew rapidly in membership and power. Templar knights, in their distinctive white mantles with a red cross, were among the most skilled fighting units of the Crusades. Non-combatant members of the Order managed a large economic infrastructure throughout Christendom, innovating financial techniques that were an early form of banking, and building fortifications across Europe and the Holy Land.

The Templars' existence was tied closely to the Crusades; when the Holy Land was lost, support for the Order faded. Rumours about the Templars' secret initiation ceremony created distrust and King Philip IV of France, deeply in debt to the Order, took advantage of the situation. In 1307, many of the Order's members in France were arrested, tortured into giving false confessions, and then burned at the stake. Under pressure from King Philip, Pope Clement V disbanded the Order in 1312. The abrupt disappearance of a major part of the European infrastructure gave rise to speculation and legends, which have kept the "Templar" name alive into the modern day.

Find links for Knights Templar here:
http://bit.ly/or3cont#knights

4 Ophites
The Ophites or Ophians (Greek Ὀφιανοί Ophianoi, from ὄφις ophis "snake") were members of a Christian

Gnostic sect depicted by Hippolytus of Rome (170–235) in a lost work, the Syntagma ("arrangement"). It is now thought that later accounts of these "Ophites" by Pseudo-Tertullian, Philastrius and Epiphanius of Salamis are all dependent on the lost Syntagma of Hippolytus. It is possible that rather than an actual sectarian name Hippolytus may have invented "Ophite" as a generic term for what he considered heretical speculations concerning the serpent of Genesis or Moses.

Apart from the sources directly dependent on Hippolytus (Pseudo-Tertullian, Philastrius and Epiphanius), Origen and Clement of Alexandria also mention the group. The group is mentioned by Irenaeus in Against Heresies (1:30).

Find links for Ophites here: http://bit.ly/or3cont#ophites

5 Fire and Stone Cut in kenjutsu

"Fire and Stone's Cut" refers to when your swords clash together. Without raising your sword, you cut as strongly as possible. This means cutting quickly with hands, body, and legs.

Find links for Fire and Stone Cut and the book of Five Rings here: http://bit.ly/or3cont#fireandstone

6 Medieval Crane on Cologne Cathedral in 1856

The foundation stone of Cologne Cathedral was laid on 15 August 1248, by Archbishop Konrad von Hochstaden. The eastern arm was completed under the direction of Master Gerhard, was consecrated in 1322 and sealed off by a temporary wall so it could be in use as the work proceeded. Eighty-four misericords in the choir date from this building phase. In the mid-4th

century work on the west front commenced under
Master Michael. This work halted in 1473, leaving the
south tower complete up to the belfry level and
crowned with a huge crane that remained in place as a
landmark of the Cologne skyline for 400 years.

Find links for Cologne Cathedral and man-powered
cranes here: http://bit.ly/or3cont#crane

Read more about Zosimyache in Vampire:
Beneficence: (Short Stories Volume III) and the
mythology behind the Ordo Lupus and the Blood Moon
Prophecy series in The Hole Inside the Earth.

Biography of Lazlo Ferran

Lazlo Ferran: Exploring the Landscapes of Truth.

Educated near Oxford, during English author Lazlo Ferran's extraordinary life, he has been an aeronautical engineering student, dispatch rider, graphic designer, full-time busker, guitarist and singer, recording two albums. Having grown up in rural Buckinghamshire Lazlo says:

"The beautiful Chiltern Hills offered the ideal playground for a child's mind, in contrast to the ultra-strict education system of Bucks."

Brought up as a Buddhist, he has travelled widely, surviving a student uprising in Athens and living for a while in Cairo, just after Sadat's assassination. Later, he spent some time in Central Asia and was only a few blocks away from gunfire during an attempt to storm the government buildings of Bishkek in 2006. He has a keen interest in theologies and philosophies of the Far East, Middle East, Asia and Eastern Europe.

After a long and successful career within the science industry, Lazlo Ferran left to concentrate on writing, to continue exploring the landscapes of truth.

From the author:

Thank you for reading my story and I hope you liked it. I value very much feedback from people and need this if each book is to be better than the last, so if you could take the time to either post a comment on my amazon page or my blog or simply email me, I would appreciate it.

Where to find Lazlo Ferran

Blog: http://www.lazloferran.com
Amazon: www.amazon.com/author/lazlo_ferran
Email: lazloferran@gmail.com